MCA
J

The Sugar Mountain Snow Ball

ELIZABETH ATKINSON

Other middle grade fiction from Islandport Press:

Cooper and Packrat:
Mystery on Pine Lake and *Mystery of the Eagle's Nest*
by Tamra Wight

Uncertain Glory
by Lea Wait

The Five Stones Trilogy:
The Fog of Forgetting and *Chantarelle*
by G. A. Morgan

Azalea, Unschooled
by Liza Kleinman

Mercy: The Last New England Vampire
by Sarah L. Thomson

The Sugar Mountain Snow Ball

ELIZABETH ATKINSON

ISLANDPORT PRESS

Islandport Press

PO Box 10

247 Portland Street

Yarmouth, ME 04096

Islandportpress.com

books@islandportpress.com

Copyright © 2015 by Elizabeth Atkinson

ISBN: 978-1-939017-71-0

Library of Congress Control Number: 2014959685

Printed in the USA by Bookmasters.

For Lisa Myers, wherever you may be.

Nothing is hopeless; we must hope for everything.
—Madeleine L'Engle, *A Wrinkle in Time*

DECEMBER

The morning I couldn't find my extra-thick striped socks turned out to be the day that changed my life.

Eleanor would say it was *serendipitous* that I couldn't find my socks, one of the huge words she likes to use. Because if I had found my socks, we never would have spent the afternoon together and discovered Madame Magnifique's sparkling poster on the community bulletin board at the used books store.

But since I spent so much time searching for my socks, I was late for school. And when you're late for school more than twice in the same month, the assistant vice principal, Mr. Tankhorn, makes you stay after for detention. So that morning happened to be my third tardy in December, even though the month had barely begun.

"See you in the cafeteria at two forty-five sharp, Ms. LaRue," said Mr. Tankhorn as I rushed through the old wooden doors of Paris Middle School seconds after the last bell.

"I apologize for being a teensy bit late again, Mr. T," I said, stomping snow off my red boots, "but I really can't stay after today. I have very important plans to"—I had to come up with something wicked smart this time, something Eleanor would say—"plans to *research* the changing cloud *formations* due to acid *reflux* and, you know, all the other *acids* and *refluxes*."

That sounded pretty good to me.

"Nice try, Ruby."

Mr. Tankhorn is the sort of person who talks stuffy, like he has wads of tissues jammed up his nose.

"The truth is, young lady," he continued, "you can go home any day of the week and text or play online games or whatever it is you kids do on the computer these days until your eyes pop out of your exploding heads. But if you cannot get to school on time, you're going to spend the afternoon with me in the cafeteria. They won't put up with these shenanigans in high school!"

The truth? Nobody in the whole school knew the truth about me, except Eleanor. I mean, they knew I was friendly, kinda short, a little plus-sized, and in the sixth grade . . . but they didn't know I did pretty much nothing after school, because I had to babysit my four-year-old twin brothers, Charlie and Henry, practically every day, since both of my parents seemed to work nonstop lately. And all the boys and I ever did was watch television game shows, sprawled across the couch, munching unsold cookies my stepmother, Mim, brought home from the café where she worked double shifts.

Our house—which is the same one my dad grew up in—is down a long, curvy driveway in a sunny clearing in the woods with a giant porch across the front of it, but it's really old and tired-looking, with the blue paint peeling off in lots of spots. I don't have my own cell phone or computer, because my parents think I'm still too young.

Plus they're always cutting corners, trying to save money. We don't even have cable or a dish, just some antenna thing that barely works. Less than twelve television channels come in, and some are smushy.

"Okay, Mr. T. See you in the cafeteria."

A couple of hours later I was standing in line with Eleanor in gym class. It was our least-favorite class, but it was the only one we had together since we were on different tracks, with Eleanor falling into the brainiac track and me in the regular track. Luckily we got to see each other at lunch too.

I bent over and whispered in her ear.

"Can I use your phone later? I know it's for emergencies, but I promise I'll be quick."

Eleanor rolled her eyes like she didn't believe me.

"Why?" she asked.

"I need to call the twins' babysitter to let her know I'll be late picking them up."

We were standing in line because that week we had to complete the President's Challenge. We're forced to do this by the government every year—an activity that, for Eleanor and me, is just another form of public embarrassment. I tend to wheeze, which comes on with a whiff of the old, moldy gym, so I really don't have the strength to do even one pull-up. And Eleanor is wicked skinny, which means she is basically weak.

So when it was our turn we pretended to try extra hard, then clutched our wrists or elbows and cried, *Ouch!*

Like always, it worked.

The gym teacher, Ms. Duncan, told us to grab ice packs and sit down on the bottom bleacher.

"Tardy again, Ruby?" whispered Eleanor as she tied her long black hair into a ponytail.

"I can't help it. All this stuff, like my extra-thick striped socks, seems to vanish into thin air. It's like our house is upside down. Pop has been on the road for three weeks now, and Mim's been leaving extra early in the morning to drop off the twins. Lately she's been working right up until supper, like ten-hour shifts—even on Saturdays—and all we ever eat is take-out from the Panda House. I'm getting sick of fried wontons and egg rolls."

"But why are your parents working so much?"

"I don't know; I guess we need the money. And also, Mim said she really wants to save up for an Aqua-Pedic aboveground pool next summer so we can float on rafts and sip pink drinks like we're in Jamaica, which would *obviously* be super fun," I sighed. "But in the meantime, I miss Pop, plus nothing's getting done. Our house is practically falling apart."

I don't want to give the wrong impression about Mim, because she would be considered the best stepmom in the entire world if she didn't have to work so many hours and do almost everything alone since my father drives freight trucks and sometimes leaves for weeks at a time. I even feel funny calling her my stepmother, since my actual mother died when I was born. Pop married Mim when I was only two years old.

Plus she has the best job, when you really think about it. Every day, Mim bakes twelve kinds of "Monster Chunk" cookies in the

Slope Side Café kitchen at the Sugar Mountain Ski Resort. After the cookies come out of the oven and cool down, she covers them in pretty plastic wrap and then seals them with this cute heart sticker that says SUGAR MOUNTAIN HOMEMADE GOODIES. The dough is Mim's super-secret recipe, and they're famous all over the East Coast—more and more stores and restaurants keep ordering them—which is why she's always so busy.

But lately I'd noticed the house seemed to be getting messier and messier every day, and we could barely close any of the overstuffed cabinets and closets, plus all of us were really tired, not just Mim, to the point where the boys and I were dozing and snoring on the couch by four p.m., especially when our very favorite TV game show, *The Price Is Right*, was extra smushy and we couldn't even make out if the contestant had won or lost.

Eleanor slipped her cell phone into my hand when we were back in the locker room, changing into our regular clothes. My wrist and her elbow had both made amazing recoveries.

"Be really quick," she said.

"Thanks," I whispered, and wedged my head into my locker, because we aren't allowed to use cell phones during school hours.

"Hello, Mrs. Petite? It's Ruby LaRue."

"You sound peculiar, dear. Is everything all right?"

"Well, not exactly. I have my head in a locker, but that's not why I'm calling. It turns out I have to stay after school today for . . . well . . . for a type of project, I guess you could say. So I'll pick up the twins a teensy bit later, if that's okay with you?"

"Oh, my. Again? Well, I suppose I'll have to take them along to the dentist," she said in her pretty old-lady way of talking that makes her sound like she's reciting poetry instead of plain old words. "But don't you worry, dear. Come on by the house after four o'clock."

Right then, Ms. Duncan blew the whistle, which meant we had to gather on the bleachers before going back to regular class and discuss what we had learned that day, like team building and cooperation and junk like that.

"*Pssht!*" Eleanor hissed as she wiggled her long, skinny finger at me to get me moving.

I peered around the corner of my locker and saw that the girls had already filed out to the bleachers.

"Thanks, Mrs. Petite. I promise to be on time tomorrow."

So after a day filled with mishaps besides my tardiness—like, I also forgot my social studies homework, and then the girl ahead of me in the lunch line got the last spicy chicken burger, and between Spanish and English classes I dropped my books in the hall, right in front of JB Knox, the most gorgeous boy in all of Paris, New Hampshire (and the star of all my daydreams)—*finally* something good happened.

I was hurrying as fast as I could to get to detention, because if you're late, then you automatically have to come back the next day for another detention, even if you're on time for school that morning. And I had promised Mrs. Petite that this wouldn't happen.

Anyway, I hurried down the halls and there it was! A sign on the cafeteria door that said ALL DETENTIONS CANCELED TODAY—NO MAKEUP DETENTION REQUIRED.

Never in my whole life had I seen a sign like that, and, believe me, I have been to a lot of detentions.

Then the next thing I knew, Eleanor silently glided around the corner and poked me in the shoulder. Except it felt more like a butterfly had landed there instead of a real poke.

"Hey, you," I said. "Don't you have Math Squad?"

"Canceled," she replied, and grinned.

"So is detention. Wonder why everything's canceled?"

"Emergency Union Reconfiguration Workshop."

"A *what* workshop?"

Sometimes Eleanor had to tell me stuff twice: the first time using the giant vocabulary words she liked to try out, and the second time, speaking normal like everyone else.

"A big meeting."

"Oh."

Then a brilliant idea-light went off in my head, telling me that *both* Eleanor and I had some free time at the same time, which almost never happened, since I babysat the twins most afternoons and her mother made her sign up for practically every brainiac activity in the school.

"Eleanor!" I grabbed her bony elbow, the one she supposedly wrenched in gym class earlier. "Let's go hang out in the village. *Ohmygosh*, wanna do that?"

I could tell she did, but—like always—needed to think about it first.

"Come on, Eleanor," I begged as we stood in the hall, the clock ticking away. "Your mother won't know. She'll think you're at Math Squad."

She squeezed her left eye shut like she really needed to concentrate.

"I promise we can go over to Wonderland's Used Books first," I said, "practically your favorite store?"

Well, that sealed the deal, because Eleanor can never resist a bookstore or the library or anything that involves the alphabet in general. So she looked right, then left, as if her mother might burst out of the walls, and then she smiled one of her special curled-up grins. And without saying another word we charged through the school doors into the frosty winter air . . . having no idea our lives would soon change forever.

"I don't think we should sit," said Eleanor.

My wheezing had begun acting up again, so I had to take a mini break on a bench and catch my breath, which surrounded me like puffs of cold smoke.

"Geez, Eleanor, relax. You act like we're being followed by the FBI."

Even though Eleanor had never met my parents, I'd had the chance to meet hers last summer at the Winterberry Festival, which takes place every year when tiny white flowers cover the winterberry bushes before the blooms turn into bright red berries. I knew Mr. and Mrs. Bandaranaike had moved a long time ago to America from an island country near India, called Sri Lanka, but they still seemed super foreign. At least her father spoke with a thick accent as he told me about the low prices at his full-service gasoline station. Her mother barely said a word and studied me like *I* looked strange, even though she wore a long, silky dress over matching pants and two shiny gold bangles on her wrist . . . something you'd never, ever see anyone wearing around here.

After arriving in this country, they had thought it would be a good idea to name their only kid after the greatest American woman they could think of—Eleanor Roosevelt—which is pretty awesome, except for the fact that Eleanor hates her name. I don't think she feels anything like an old lady who was married to a president a million years ago.

"I'm so starving I'm about to eat my tongue!" I said, still wheezing a bit between each word. "Let's take a teeny-tiny detour and get a mocha ripple milkshake at The Avalanche."

"Ruby, you promised—the bookstore first," said Eleanor. "Besides, tongue is chewy. You wouldn't like it."

"Yuck! Who would eat a tongue?"

"Duck tongue is a delicacy throughout many parts of Asia."

"Ducks have tongues?"

"Apparently, and they are very tasty to some people," she giggled, "but I wouldn't know. We are pescatarians."

"Pesca-whats?"

"Fish-eating vegetarians."

Eleanor and her giant words.

"I don't care what you call it, Eleanor, but whatever you eat, it smells better than *anything* in the whole cafeteria when you bring your lunch from home. And if you didn't act so stubborn, your folks would have me over for dinner so I could try some of it."

"I've already told you," said Eleanor, "eating a meal at my house is the same as testifying in front of a jury."

Even though we had been best friends since we were in the same fourth-grade class, neither of us had been to the other's home. It was mostly because Eleanor's mom had so many rules for her and scheduled almost every moment of her life. But I also felt there was more to it, as if Eleanor didn't want anyone to get to know her family.

"Your mother can't be *that* bad, Eleanor," I said. "The problem is, you're *too* good, and FYI, being perfect is very harmful if you've read anything about it. We went over it in health class. You can get eating disorders and cold sores and depression and joint pain and all sorts of stuff from trying to be perfect. Look at me. I don't have any of those problems, and you know why?"

She crossed her arms and rolled her eyes. "Why, Ruby?"

"Because I know trying to be perfect is practically the worst thing you can do!"

We arrived in the center of Paris a little past three o'clock. And when I'm talking about "Paris," it isn't that city over in France, although sometimes I wish it were, because it would be more than unbelievably cool if I were a French kid living in Paris.

But our Paris is pretty special, too. It's this old-fashioned New England village that Mim says looks exactly like something Norman Rockwell, the artist, could have painted. It's tucked deep into the eastern side of the White Mountains in New Hampshire, where almost everything is connected to skiing and snowboarding in the winter, which neither Eleanor nor I have ever tried. It's just way too expensive for most people who live around here.

Our main ski resort is Sugar Mountain, and you can literally walk to the entrance from Winterberry Common, which is an enormous square park plunked in the middle of town, where the annual festival takes place. The common is surrounded by tons of cute shops and restaurants and fun places to browse. And since it's a touristy ski town, a lot of the business owners string cheerful white lights around the windows, so it seems like every single day is some kind of national holiday, even when it isn't.

Well, Eleanor and I hadn't been two minutes inside Wonderland's Used Books when she did her *pssht* noise again, to get my attention.

"*Quoi?*"

That's French for "What?," and is pronounced *kwa*, with a little gaggy sound in the back of your throat. Pretty much anybody with deep roots in this part of New Hampshire is French-Canadian, like my stepmom and my pop, who can trace both of their families back to Québec, Canada.

"*This!*"

Eleanor pointed at a sparkly poster on the bulletin board, so I stuck my favorite celebrity magazine, *Famous & Fabulous*, back on the shelf and tiptoed over.

"Look!" she said, twitching and hopping like she was really excited, which was *very* unusual for Eleanor.

I gasped.

"*Madame Magnifique?* That must be French for Mrs. Magnificent. I've never heard of Madame Magnifique. Have you, Eleanor?"

Eleanor squinted and lowered her voice.

"No. But I have heard about the powers of astrological clairvoyants."

"Of *astro-clare-whats?* It says she's a psychic. You know, like those television commercials they have on right before dinner, where you can call this lady named Venus in Las Vegas on the phone and ask her if you can speak to your dead uncle or find out if your boyfriend is going to propose?"

Eleanor's face dropped.

"She's not that kind of psychic, Ruby."

"What do you mean? What kind is she?"

"Keep your voice down," she said, peering over the shelves. "I don't want anyone to hear this."

We turned our backs and faced the window so no one in the store could read our lips.

"A long time ago, my father told me about a visionary his family knew when he was a boy back in Sri Lanka. She lived alone on the highest peak in the jungle. A very old astrologist who not only interpreted birth charts, she *saw* dreams—a person's dreams."

"Wait, wait, wait!" I said. "Back up to birth charts. What's that?"

"It's complicated, but basically it's a recording of the alignment and energy of the planets at the moment you're born. Some people refer to birth charts when analyzing their personality or weighing events like marriage or predicting future challenges. But you need a trained astrologist to interpret them. Get it?"

"Sort of, I guess. So the astrologist tells you what your dreams mean, too?"

"No, no, not at all. They do consider our past lives, but that's not what I'm talking about."

"*Past lives?* Like if you used to be a princess, or a famous actress?"

"That's not what I am talking about either," she said, and rubbed her forehead like she was thinking extra hard. "Ruby, listen to me. This astrologist, whom my father knew, did not *see* ordinary dreams you have when you sleep. What she saw was your deepest longings in life, impossible dreams you only dared hope would come true . . . just as it says here on the poster."

Until that moment I had never, ever thought about what Eleanor dreamed. I had assumed she didn't have time to dream, since she was so busy with scheduled activities.

Me? I dreamed like it was my job—like, if I could pick a dream job for life, it would be "dreamer," or something like that. I was dripping with dreams.

"*Wow,*" was all I could say . . . just as impressed by Eleanor's brilliant thoughts as by her stories of ancient stuff on the other side of the world.

"And Ruby! They called her *Vishishta.*"

At this point her eyes grew even wider.

"*Double wow,*" I whispered a little louder this time. "That's a very mysterious-sounding name!"

"More than that. This is a Sinhalese word, which translates closely to *magnificent*."

We stared at each other, our mouths open in amazement, because this had to be more than a mere coincidence. The very fact that we both had the afternoon off together *and* happened to see this poster offering a one-day-only *free* reading by a mind reader *just like* the one who lived near Eleanor's father, like, fifty years ago on the other side of the world—and with practically the same name! Well, that's something you do NOT ignore.

Except right then, three perfect girls (dressed in frosty pink and white furry jackets) and two perfect boys crossed the street, and all of a sudden I forgot what we were talking about . . . *An Outers sighting!* The first ones of the season.

In case you don't know, Outers are very rich, very happy, very beautiful people, from some faraway place, who fill Paris in the winter months like the delicious cream in the middle of an éclair. Always perfectly dressed and perfectly smiling, Outers are the happiest, coolest people on Earth. And these perfect people choose to ski and snowboard at Sugar Mountain.

"*Ohmygosh*, Eleanor, look at them. They're sooo . . . *perfect*." I sighed deeply. "Do you think we'll ever get to go to the Snow Ball?"

The Sugar Mountain Snow Ball is the end-of-the-ski-season glam fest on the last Saturday of March, attended by all the Outers and a few lucky locals in Paris with money and connections.

"*The Snow Ball?*"

If I didn't know Eleanor as well as I did, I'd say she almost sounded angry.

"Ruby, I have to be home in thirty-two minutes. This psychic lady is free today only. And don't you remember what you just told me about how perfection can be harmful?"

The Outers had crossed the street and disappeared into Chez Neige, one of the fanciest, trendiest ski boutiques that practically no one from Paris, New Hampshire, can afford.

"But, Eleanor, don't you wish you were one of them?"

"You know nothing about them," she replied as she studied the poster, "only what they appear to be, roaming through town in ostentatious clumps."

"I guess you're right. I get so obsessed sometimes—the same way I do about a gorgeous charm necklace or a new kind of candy bar—that I think I'm going to lose my mind if I don't get to—"

"Wait a minute, Ruby, look at this."

"What?"

"At the bottom of the poster, it says: *Located on Apparition Way, the alley beyond Wonderland's Used Books.* Where is that?"

I had never noticed an alley behind Wonderland's, or heard of a street called Apparition Way, and I knew this town like I knew the *TV Guide* schedule.

"It must be a typo."

Eleanor smiled one of her curly smirks and said, "C'mon, let's find Madame Magnifique!"

I was shocked. Eleanor was never daring. She always thought everything over slowly and carefully to make sure she wouldn't get in trouble.

"But you only have, like, thirty minutes left, and anyway, what if someone sees you sneaking around in some spooky dark alley and tells your parents?"

"I don't care. I have to do this, Ruby."

And before I knew it, she was gone.

Eleanor raced along the snowy sidewalk like a contestant on one of those reality shows where you have to be the first one to find some clue that leads to some other clue or you're out of the game.

I moved more slowly, slipping all over the place, until I fell flat on my bum.

"Wait up! It's not like she's going to vanish if we don't find her today."

"I see it, Ruby," she said, waving. "It's right here. Hurry!"

I rolled over onto my knees and stood up, although it was hard to balance on the super-slippery sidewalk. When I finally caught up to her, Eleanor squealed and pointed at the back wall of a brick building where an old wooden sign was nailed to the corner.

"*Ap-pa-ri-tion* Way," I read out loud, then peered down the narrow road. "I wonder why we've never noticed it before?"

Suddenly Eleanor scrambled up and over the mound of crusty snow.

"Whoa! There's no *way* I'm going down there," I said. "It's too deep."

"But Ruby, I see a door with a light up ahead. Come on—it's not that far."

I took one step and immediately broke straight through the packed snow past my red boots to the middle of my orange leggings. Eleanor, on the other hand, scurried across the surface like a rabbit.

"This is *crazy*, Eleanor! Why isn't this plowed if it's a real alley?"

I trudged down the tiny street, hoisting one leg out of the packed drifts as the other one plunged through to the bottom. Eventually I caught up to Eleanor, who was gazing at an open door. My wheezing had really kicked in, so I took a moment to catch my breath again.

"Is this it?" I puffed.

But before she could reply, a head with a mountain of white hair appeared sideways in the doorway.

"*Bonjour!*"

Neither of us said anything.

"*Bonjour, bonjour, les filles!*" the head greeted us again.

Eleanor gawked at the woman like she was staring at a ghost.

"*Bonjour* to you too," I said, since I knew some French. "Are you the psychic lady?"

"*Oui, oui*, indeed, I am," she replied with a glamorous accent. "All *rrrr*eadings free today. And let me see, you must be—?"

"Ruby," I said, "like the color of a rose. But I bet you already knew that, huh?"

"*Non*, I don't believe we've met before."

She definitely wasn't the kind of psychic they showed on television ads. Those psychics knew everything about you just from talking to you on the phone.

Madame Magnifique turned to Eleanor, who continued to stare like she was in some sort of trance.

"And who is your silent friend?"

"This is Eleanor. She's kinda quiet at first, until she gets to know you."

"*Bien! S'il vous plaît*, come in, girls. *Vite, vite!* I have much to tell you."

Madame Magnifique was very round, and almost as short as I was. Her fancy white dress dragged across the ground, and a thick sparkly shawl kept her shoulders warm. She wore fuzzy white gloves with rings slipped over each finger, and on her feet were cherry-colored boots that looked exactly like something a fairy godmother would wear. Strangest of all, a long red feather poked out of her curly white hair.

After slipping off our boots, we followed her through a narrow hallway (which smelled like warm gingerbread) to a square room shimmering in golden light. Thick, soft velvet covered every inch of the space: velvet curtains, velvet furniture, and a velvet cloth draped over the round table in the middle of the room. Even the carpet felt like velvet beneath our socks.

"Holy ravioli," I said, "this is *wicked* cool."

"Please sit," said Madame M. "Be comfortable."

Our chairs were so low, my shoulders pressed against the edge of the table, while Madame M perched high on a stool across from us. She said nothing as she lit two tall candles in the center of the table. It all felt very serious.

"You know what this reminds me of?" I whispered to Eleanor, who looked like she'd seen a ghost. "That movie with the boy who ate too many tacos and saw flying dragons; do you remember that? The part where the—"

"*Excusez-moi!*" said Madame M. "There is not much time. I have a manicure appointment in fifteen minutes."

Right then Eleanor looked at me—her eyes bulging out of her head—because I knew, on top of being scared, she suddenly remembered the time and didn't want to get in trouble with her mother for being late. I searched the room for a clock, but before I could find one, Madame M began to hum loudly. She gazed up at the ceiling and stretched her arms over her puffy white head and red feather. Then all at once, she stopped her humming and arm-waving and slapped her hands on top of the table.

I glanced at Eleanor and could tell she had already forgotten about the time.

"*Maintenant, les filles:* You must place your hands flat and lock your thumbs like this."

We immediately copied her, our hands shaped like those bird shadows you make on the wall.

"Now, close your eyes tightly and say these words: *Stars and moons and worlds that beam, lead me to my deepest drrream!*"

I had to force myself not to giggle as we repeated the funny chant.

"*Ouvrez!*" she cried, and blew out the candles. "Open!"

The sweet smoke clouded the space in front of us as Madame M squeezed the top of our bird hands at the same time.

"You!" she said, studying Eleanor. "Once your creativity is unleashed, there will be no stopping you from realizing your fullest potential and achieving your deepest *drrream*."

Eleanor's mouth dropped open in amazement.

"And you!" she said, facing me. "In order to unlock your deepest *drrream*, you must go outside your world, to the unfamiliar, reaching far beyond your comfort zone."

Now *I* was amazed, like she really could see into our minds.

Madame Magnifique lifted her hands and blew across her palms as if scattering magical dust. Then she smacked them together and back and forth like she was trying to wipe off the extra magic.

"And girls . . . if this does not come true within four months, come back and see me. I'll give you a refund."

"But it was free?" I reminded her.

"It was?" said the psychic. "What a bargain!"

We followed her back through the narrow hallway (that still smelled like warm gingerbread) and stumbled out of the alley door into the late-afternoon light. I felt a little dazed, like I had just woken up from a deep sleep.

"Thank you," we mumbled at the exact same time.

Madame M smiled as she gave a tiny wave with the tips of her fingers.

"*Rêvez bien!* Dream well, Ruby and Eleanor."

As soon as Madame M shut the door with a thud, my heart began to pound. I was so excited I practically screamed, because I knew *exactly* what her reading had meant, and I couldn't wait to get Eleanor's opinion.

"Eleanor! *Ohmygosh*, ELEANOR!"

But Eleanor didn't turn around. She was already darting back across the mounds of snow toward the street.

"You have to slow down, Eleanor. This snow is way too soft for me."

I managed to find my tracks from before, but this time I was sinking even deeper, which made me even slower, and made my breathing raspier from all this crazy rushing around.

"I need to hurry, Ruby—I'm late."

Now I could see only the top half of her body behind the snowbank at the end of the alley.

"But what about our psychic readings? Was that freaky or what? And Madame M was *so* good; she read my mind like my head was a crystal ball!"

Eleanor bobbed up and down, glancing back and forth like she was expecting to see her mother leading a search party.

"We'll talk tomorrow."

"But, El—"

"I *really* have to go," she called. "See you at school."

And just like that, she disappeared. Our one free afternoon together had ended.

My orange leggings were so damp and freezing as I walked home that I could barely feel my legs, making my excitement grow colder too. I knew what I wanted to do about Madame M's dream reading, but I wasn't absolutely sure without first talking it over with Eleanor. And when I thought about that very thing—talking stuff over with Eleanor—I realized I *never* got to talk stuff over with her. We only talked between classes in the crowded hallways, or sitting on the bleachers in gym class, faking injuries, or during lunch, where we were always surrounded by the Math Squad boys, who drooled all over Eleanor, even though she had no idea they all liked her—especially that Anton Orlov. He was so in love with Eleanor that he couldn't stop insulting everyone around her, especially me.

It didn't seem fair that her mother forced her to do all these special activities and classes, and then run home instantly every single day. I had never heard of anyone who had so many rules and chores and lessons, like the cello, not to mention all the other junk she had to sign up for.

The funny thing is, she was never expected to work at her father's gas station. If kids had any extra time to do anything around here, they would work, especially if their families owned businesses. But Eleanor said her *thaththa* (which is "Dad" in their Sinhala language) told her she had the rest of her life to worry about making money; he believed childhood was the time to learn and explore. The problem was, her *amma* (which is "Mom") told her what to learn and where to explore. And none of it ever included me.

On my way home, I had to stop again and catch my breath. For some reason, my wheezing had been acting up more than usual lately. I rested against the tall iron fence in front of the town's only mansion near the far end of Maine Street, at the corner of Bon Hiver Lane. Mim had told me that the people who built the giant stone house back in the 1800s were rich railroad folks, and their relatives had lived there for more than a hundred years, until the train business went belly-up and they moved away.

All I know is, I'd never seen a bigger front yard in my entire life, except in pictures of those humongous castles over in France. Come to think of it, this mansion reminded me of a real French castle with its tower at each end, and an enormous rectangular section in the middle with lots and lots of windows.

After the train family left for good, other millionaires bought and sold it, but no one ever knew who they were—probably rich Outers who wanted somewhere to ski. But since the economy had been bad for a while now, that old mansion had been sitting empty. Until today.

In the distance, beyond the front yard, an eighteen-wheeler (the kind Pop drove) was backed up behind the house with several guys moving furniture down the ramp. I pressed my face between the cold metal bars to see if there were kids or dogs or horses or anything interesting.

And that's when I saw him.

A boy stood way over to the left side of the property, far from all the commotion. He was even taller than Eleanor, and skinnier, too, and I mean stick-figure skinny, like someone who doesn't even *like* food. He had a mess of brown hair hanging down around his face, and I think he wore glasses—it was hard to tell from so far away. His baggy green jacket came down to his knees and it was unzipped, even though a cold wind blew down from the mountains.

He peered at me through a pair of binoculars like he was a spy, so I jammed my arms through the fence and waved, pretending to surrender.

"I give up! Come on over and arrest me."

But instead of laughing, the boy dropped his binoculars like he thought it was a real holdup.

"Sorry, I'm only goofin' around," I yelled. "What's your name?"

I couldn't tell if he could hear me or if I had truly scared him, because all of a sudden he turned and took off around the corner of one of those towers. It seemed like everyone was running away from me today.

"Charlie! Quit touching every cookie chunk with your nasty little hands. And Henry, move your melon head so I can see the television, mister."

My little brothers and I were sprawled on the couch, watching *The Price Is Right*. The reruns of the original version are shown every day from three to five p.m. on channel 6. The old ones hosted by Bob Barker are, in my opinion, far better than the newer versions. And the prices don't make sense anyway, whether the show was filmed thirty years ago or yesterday. I don't know where the contestants do their shopping, but Mim says everything is wacky out in California, where they play the game, which is probably why the prices are nothing like ours.

The three of us were hanging out as usual, gobbling down yesterday's leftover Monster Chunk cookies from the Slope Side Café, since it was almost dinnertime and we were practically starving to death. Mrs. Petite had been taking a nap when I picked up the twins, because her tooth ached from whatever the dentist had done. And Mr. Petite was busy painting his duck decoys on the dining-room table, so the boys hadn't eaten a thing since lunch other than butter cream mints from the candy bowl. And, of course, Eleanor and I never had gotten to The Avalanche for that mocha ripple milkshake.

"Two seventy-five is wrong! Three ninety-eight is the correct answer!" yelled Bob Barker as the *too bad* music played on the TV. "Oh, *too bad*, Louise—but thanks for playing."

"Three ninety-eight?" I complained out loud. "Where do they buy their pretzels? At the jewelry store?"

That made the twins crack up and repeat my words. They were always copying everything I said.

"I don't want any more cookies," announced Charlie, who was stretched out in Pop's recliner, having won the honor five minutes earlier by beating Henry at stuffing the most Monster Chunks in his mouth. "I want egg rolls!"

"We're not having Chinese take-out for dinner tonight," I said, and sat up, which startled our old cat, Marilyn Monroe. She jumped to the ground and wandered off to the other end of the house in search of quiet. "Mim said she'd pick up fried chicken for a change."

Charlie whined, "I don't like chicken," just as my stepmom burst through the front door, toting about thirteen bags. She can carry more plastic grocery sacks than any other human on earth. No matter how many are in the car, she never makes more than one trip lugging them into the house.

"Too late, sweetie," said Mim as she dumped everything, including two greasy cardboard buckets, onto our kitchen table. "I have enough chicken here to feed the whole neighborhood."

Henry leaned forward and scratched himself all over, the deep-fried smell waking him like an alarm clock.

My stepmom smiled like always, but I could tell she was tired.

"I'll get the soda," I offered, as Mim lowered herself into a kitchen chair and sighed.

"Thanks, Rosebud—and turn the channel to *Hollywood Crime Watch*, would you please?"

She didn't even put the groceries away, just shoved them aside, and then pulled out the take-out paper plates, plastic forks and knives, and a pile of napkins. Both boys dug into supper like they hadn't eaten in days.

"So what did you kids do this afternoon?" asked Mim, frosting a biscuit with butter before sliding it into her mouth.

Right then, I worried the boys would blurt out something about their visit to the dentist with Mrs. Petite, but they were so busy chomping, they didn't hear a thing.

"Nothing much—the usual," I replied, even though I was *dying* to tell her all about the mysterious Madame M and our psychic readings.

But my stepmother would have wondered why I was off running around town and not home watching the boys, which would have involved confessing my frequent tardiness, where it all began. Also, I wasn't so sure she would agree with the way I saw my reading, which had me so excited that I couldn't wait to see Eleanor tomorrow in gym class and get her take on it.

I peeled the crunchy skin off a wing, the best part, and ate it first.

"I want more soda with my chicken," said Charlie.

"*May* I have more soda, *please*," corrected Mim. "And I thought you just said you didn't like chicken."

"Is Pop coming home this weekend?" I asked.

"I don't think so," sighed Mim. "He picked up another delivery that pays such good money he couldn't turn it down. But someone needs to get up on this roof and shovel it before it caves into the attic. I've never seen so much snow this early."

The Green Gobster came on the TV, one of the boys' favorite shows. They jumped off their seats and back onto the couch, hollering, "Louder than THUNDER, who, do you WONDER? Green Gobster!"

Mim yawned, then gulped her entire glass of root beer in one big chug.

"Oh my, I missed the end of *Hollywood Crime Watch* again," she said. "I'm so exhausted, I'm gonna hit the hay, Ruby. Can you make sure the boys change into their pj's during a commercial, in case they fall asleep on the couch?"

All at once, something about that didn't feel right to me. It seemed like Mim should be going to bed after us, not before. And that Pop should be home by now. But instead of saying anything, I hugged my stepmom good night and opened the dessert cabinet over the sink.

"Okay, boys. Who wants whoopie pies and who wants kettle corn?"

The only class that Eleanor and I shared, gym class, met second period, three times a week. On a good day, which was rare, we got to play whatever we wanted, and we always chose Ping-Pong. But today was the horrible continuation of the President's Challenge.

"For your age group," announced Ms. Duncan, "I need to see twenty-seven solid body curls, nose to knees, without stopping." She always hollered like she was giving lifesaving directions for an emergency. "Pair up and count off for each other!"

"Pair up?" I repeated, smiling at Eleanor. "My two favorite words, right after *Sit down* and *Time's up*."

I collapsed onto the hard floor with a thud. Eleanor folded down onto the exercise mat as easily as a piece of tissue and crossed her long brown legs.

"We have to talk about yesterday," I whispered. "I don't know about you, but I could barely sleep, thinking about Madame M's dream advice."

Eleanor began curling first, or at least pretending to curl.

"I mean, mine was so obvious," I said, "about *reaching far beyond my comfort zone and going outside my own world*. Somehow she knew I dream more than anything of being an Outer! Being perfectly happy and pretty and smart and having incredible clothes and going to the Snow Ball, hopefully with JB Knox. So, Eleanor, I've been thinking about it all night, and I know exactly what I have to do!"

"You do?" asked Eleanor, breathing heavily, like she was actually doing the curls.

"It's so obvious. I have to start skiing! Or maybe snowboarding. No, I think skiing makes more sense."

Eleanor's back dropped and her head hit the floor.

"Wait! Are you really trying to do these sit-ups?" I asked. "I haven't been counting, you know."

"*Ski*, Ruby? You don't know how to ski. But, more importantly, how can you be an Outer if the most fundamental principle of being an Outer is living *out* of town?"

"I even thought of that. I could be the very first Outer who lived *in* town, and maybe even start a branch of Outers called the Inners, or something like that. Maybe you could join too."

Eleanor stared at me, then shook her head in that way she does when she can't seem to figure out how the real world works.

"I know skiing is super expensive and I don't have any of the equipment and I would probably need a lesson or two, but Eleanor, it makes so much sense. Madame M practically said so."

"SIX minutes left, people!" Ms. Duncan roared. "Change partners if you haven't already. When I blow my whistle you must *stop* immediately, get in line, and report your results to me."

It was my turn even though I knew I could barely do one sit-up. I didn't have the build for it.

"Skiing may not be as impossible as my dream," Eleanor mumbled as she held my feet. "To tell you the truth, I can't stop thinking about her astonishing predictions either."

"*And?*"

I had actually managed to do three curls, but then I could feel my wheezing flare up.

"Did she read right through you, too, or what?"

"Yes. She did."

"So spill it," I gasped, and sat up to listen since the gym was so noisy. "What did she mean by saying all that stuff about your creative side?"

"Well, you know what I love doing more than anything else in the world, Ruby."

It was pretty obvious what Eleanor loved, since she constantly doodled and sketched pictures in her binders.

"Drawing?"

"Partly, but what am I always drawing?"

I began twisting back and forth a little to catch my breath.

"Umm, let me think. I don't know, mostly pictures of people in gorgeous clothes, I guess."

"Exactly—*haute couture!* I'm passionate about *every* aspect of designing clothes—sketching, cutting, sewing, fabric—and especially the thought of people wearing my original creations."

As I twisted to the right, I noticed a group of older boys studying a poster on the other side of the gym.

"Do you mean you wanna work for one of those high-end, expensive stores at the mall?"

"More than that, Ruby—I want to create my own fashion line!"

But I had stopped listening to Eleanor, because standing directly across the gym from us was the cutest boy in all of Paris.

"*Ohmygosh!* Tell me that's JB Knox."

Eleanor frowned, then turned and squinted. I knew I had interrupted her dream reading, but this was way too important—a JB sighting!

"Yep," she mumbled, "it's him."

JB and I didn't cross paths that often, since he was a whole year ahead of us, so seeing him during one of my classes was like a freak occurrence.

"I don't know why you like JB, Ruby. He's arrogant, strident, domineering, and, worst of all, callous."

"*What are you talking about?* He's hot!"

Eleanor shook her head.

"A boy like that uses everyone else as a mirror, seeing only his own reflection."

I felt kinda sorry for Eleanor, because, frankly, she had little social experience and didn't understand the way relationships worked. But right now, I had no time to explain any of it to her.

"Can you tell if JB is looking this way?"

"I don't know, Ruby. Look for yourself."

"I can't *look*. I don't want him to see me looking at him if he's looking at me."

Eleanor groaned.

"He's looking at some poster."

I twisted back and peered over.

"I wonder what they're doing here?"

"Maybe the seventh grade has gym next."

"But that would mean they're early."

"Are you done faking curls, or what?" asked Eleanor. "Our time is almost up."

"Even from way over here, JB's cuter than cute, don't you think?" I sighed. "He's like an Outer, except technically he can't be one either."

Eleanor grabbed my shoulders and stared into my eyes.

"Ruby! Snap out of it! He's a whole year older than you. He plays starting center on the middle school basketball team . . . and he has a fan club of *cheerleaders*."

The whistle blew and everyone ran over to line up in front of Ms. Duncan. I stuck my hand in the air for Eleanor to help me stand.

"You know what your problem is?" I asked as we walked over to join the others. "And I mean this in the nicest possible way, Eleanor: You're too glass half-empty."

"Whatever," she said, and scrunched up her face. "By the way, you did three sit-ups and I did nine."

"So let's say I did twenty-seven and you did thirty-three. See? Glass half-full!"

"That isn't optimism," replied Eleanor, "that's lying. But at least my mother doesn't care about gym class."

We stood in line to report our little fibs to the president. Ms. Duncan gripped her clipboard as if recording the number of people missing during a snowslide.

"Final count, girls?"

"Well," I began, the way I always do in gym, "since I started to wheeze a bit, I completed only the minimum of twenty-seven, but Eleanor beat me and did thirty-three, and probably could have kept on going."

Ms. Duncan switched her gaze over to Eleanor and raised one eyebrow.

"Maybe you can demonstrate your curling expertise for the class, Ms. Bandaranaike?"

"Oh, she should probably wait a week or two," I suggested. "Give her stomach muscles time to recover."

Eleanor nudged me, which meant she wanted me to stop talking, but it didn't matter because right then the five-minute warning bell rang and Ms. Duncan told everyone to go change.

"JB and those boys are gone now," I whispered. "Let's see what that poster says."

"*Ruby*, I need to hurry. I wore tights today."

"It'll only take a second."

I dragged Eleanor over to the far wall, where we found a big sign-up sheet. The second I read it, I gasped.

"*Ski club!* And JB signed his name. Don't you know what this means?"

"It means a public school in a ski resort town where it snows seven months of the year is finally sponsoring a club for its own citizens who can't afford to ski," she sighed, and leaned her back against the wall.

"No, Eleanor, that's glass half-empty again."

Now I grabbed *her* shoulders.

"It means Madame M's prediction—*my very deepest dream*—is coming true!"

Just then, Eleanor's eyes popped out of her head. I turned to see what she was looking at and nearly fainted. Standing right behind me was JB Knox.

"Hey," he smiled, and pointed at the floor. "I forgot my backpack."

I tried to think of something—*anything*—to say, but my tongue was tied. I stared at the backpack as Eleanor reached down to get it.

"Thanks," said JB, and he smiled again as Eleanor handed it to him, then jogged off toward the locker room.

"Bye, JB!" I finally managed to blurt.

"See ya later," he called back, before disappearing through the door marked BOYS.

Eleanor crossed her arms, rolled her eyes, and shook her head.

"What did I tell you?" I said. "Glass half-full!"

Just as Mim had said, I, too, could not remember a year when there had been so much snow so early in the winter. Walking home that day after school, I realized it had to be Mother Nature's way of pushing me to take up skiing. Plus, running into JB—who actually promised to *see me later*—left no doubt in my mind. Every little sign so far seemed to be leading me to my dream of becoming an Outer and going to the Snow Ball with the cutest boy in all of Paris—and if Eleanor and I hadn't visited Madame M, I never would have seen my own destiny jumping out at every corner.

Like a lot of parents and older people in town, my pop grew up skiing at Sugar Mountain, before a big company bought it and turned it into a fancy resort and, according to him, made it a destination for snobby, rich people. It was true about the rich part. Like Eleanor had said, most kids in Paris couldn't afford to buy a lift ticket, let alone all the equipment and the designer ski clothes. Pop said he used to get hand-me-down skis from the neighbors and lift tickets were pretty cheap, and no one cared if you wore an old snowmobile jacket and a pair of jeans.

But I have to admit, I didn't see anything snobby about the people who skied. They couldn't help it if they were completely happy and lived life like it was a fun party where you got to dress up every day and hang around with your awesomely cool friends.

Obviously, skiing had to be in my blood, since my father was practically an expert when he was younger. And, anyway, how hard could it be? I knew I wasn't the most athletic person on the planet, but even I could stand on two skinny strips of wood or plastic, lean on two poles, and glide down a hill, with gravity doing all the work.

Eleanor *had* convinced me, however, that I should probably be on the safe side and take a lesson or two before joining the ski club. But my one big problem was finding the time and the money, on top of convincing Mim to let me ski. I guess that was more than one problem, but I was still determined to figure it out, because it was an important step in fulfilling my deepest dream and ultimate destiny of becoming an Outer and going to the Snow Ball with JB.

At the end of Maine Street, before I turned down Bon Hiver Lane toward the Petites' home to pick up the twins, I stopped and stared through the mansion fence. That place really did remind me of a castle, as if the king and queen of Paris lived there, perched at the end of the boulevard that ran from the center of town. I crammed my nose between the black iron posts and counted the windows: eighteen normal-size ones, six tall ones, and four that stuck out in a half-circle, not to mention all the round windows up and down the two towers. And that was only the front of the house.

The whole property looked abandoned again—no cars, trucks, or even a worker anywhere in sight—but then I thought to myself that maybe that boy was playing somewhere inside the mansion.

I decided to walk over and knock on the door. After all, it was just a house where a kid like me lived. So I dropped my backpack to the ground and tried to lift the giant latch, but it was locked. That's when I noticed a tiny metal door on the right stone post, so I opened it. Inside was a button, like a doorbell. I pressed it long and hard in case it didn't work too well, like our doorbell. Then I waited a few seconds for someone to walk down the driveway and let me in.

"No one's home," came a boy's voice from inside the metal box.

It startled me, so it took me a second to reply.

"If no one's home, how come you're talking?"

Silence. Then the voice spoke again.

"It's illogical, but that's what I'm supposed to say when my parents aren't here."

"*Hey*, wait a sec. How can you hear me if you're inside your house?"

"The technology is a basic intercom system dating back to the 1950s."

"Cool! So, I'm Ruby LaRue—what's your name?"

Nothing came out of the box for a few seconds. Then: "Please, go away."

Go away? No one had ever said that to me, except for a few times when we were assigned group projects and I tried to be part of a group with kids who didn't include anyone other than their friends, or the brainiacs who would do all the work for them.

"Well, just so you know," I told him, "you can come over to *my* house anytime and hang out with me and my brothers and watch TV if you're lonely in there. My stepmom works at the Slope Side Café over at Sugar Mountain, so we've got every kind of Monster Chunk cookie they make."

I waited a minute, in case he needed to think it over.

"Hello?" I called into the metal box. "Are you there?"

I sighed and picked up my backpack, but I wasn't ready to give up yet. I decided I would try again the next day, and maybe the day after that. I mean, honestly, who doesn't want a friend?

By the time I picked up the twins at Mrs. Petite's house and got them home, *The Price Is Right* had started. We plopped on the couch and ate cookie leftovers and drank soda. The boys had a burping contest, which Charlie always wins, since he's louder and grosser than Henry. That meant Charlie got to sit in Pop's recliner once again for the rest of the afternoon, which was fine with me, since I was wicked sleepy.

All I wanted to do was think about how I could reach my dream goal. But the more I thought about it, lying on the couch and munching Monster Chunks, like I did every afternoon, the more I wanted to take a nap.

A few days later, the three of us were sitting on the couch in the exact same spots, eating broken cookies and sipping soda, when the TV screen popped without warning. So now we had absolutely nothing to do except stare at the black screen. And I wasn't one inch closer to my dream.

If anything, I'd begun to worry it would never happen.

The phone rang and I glanced over at the caller ID.

Eleanor? Eleanor never called unless it had something to do with official school business, like a bake sale to raise money for the Math Squad. She wasn't allowed to just chat on the phone. Plus, I thought she had her cello lesson today.

"LaRue residence," I blurted into the handset. "I saw your name, Eleanor, and couldn't help myself. Did that sound like something an Outer would say?"

"Ruby! There's no time for your delusional Outer aberrations. Amma is gone."

"What?!" I gasped. "Your mother is *gone* gone?"

"YES!"

"You mean, she's *dead?*"

"No, no, no!" cried Eleanor. And then suddenly she started giggling. And giggling and giggling, more and more, until she must have dropped the phone, because I could have sworn I heard it fall on the floor.

"Eleanor? *Eleanor?*"

She was laughing really hard now, the kind of laugh that cramps your stomach and fills your eyes with tears.

"I'm coming over there, Eleanor, if you don't tell me what's going on! Are you losing your marbles? Or has someone taken you hostage and drugged you? Are you calling me from the closet?"

"*Stop!*" she shrieked, picking up the phone again and giggling hysterically one more time. "Oh, Ruby—I think Madame Magnifique may really be right."

"What are you talking about?"

"The unattainable now seems feasible! Even though I wasn't able to locate her on my way home from school."

"Locate who?"

"Madame Magnifique," she cried. "The alley, Apparition Way—it's deserted now, and blocked by Dumpsters. Even the street sign is gone."

"Okay. You aren't making any sense, Eleanor. I think I should hang up and dial 911."

"I swear, Ruby, nothing's wrong. The opposite is true! At this very moment, Thaththa is driving Amma to the airport. I got an emergency call from my parents as I was walking home from school. My mother had to leave unexpectedly for our old neighborhood in New York to take care of my great-aunt, Nenda Soma, who's in the hospital."

"I'm so confused," I said. "What's the good part of all this?"

Eleanor groaned like she did when she felt everything was so obvious, but no one else got it.

"My. Mother. Is. Away. *And* my cello lesson has been canceled!"

A few seconds passed in silence as I tried to figure out what in the world Eleanor was . . . and then it hit me like a six-foot icicle.

"Ohhhhhh!" I yelled into the phone. "You're completely *alone?*"

"Alone and *unsupervised*, with nothing to do for the rest of the afternoon. Well, nothing I *must* do. There's plenty I *want* to do. I don't know where to begin. I've dreamed of this moment all my life."

That's when I heard a crash behind me. The twins were on the floor.

"Charlie!" I yelled. "Get off Henry and play nice, you two."

"What's going on over there?" asked Eleanor. "I thought your brothers were lazy and easy to babysit. Are they fighting?"

"Not really, but the television made this popping noise and went black a few minutes ago and we're already going batty. There's nothing to do. I called Mim right after it blew, and she said we could go to the playground at the Winterberry Common if I could find a friend to help me keep an eye on these two, but it's cold and it'll be dark soon, plus the snow is deep, so I don't know who would want to go."

Without mulling it over like she always does, Eleanor squealed, "I do!"

It took forever to get Charlie and Henry dressed in their snow gear, and I couldn't find their hats. They hated hats anyway, so they had probably hidden them and just weren't telling me.

By the time we finally arrived at Winterberry Common, Eleanor was waiting for us at a picnic table, bent over a pad of paper, drawing. Fingerless gloves kept at least part of her hands warm. Even though it was cold and windy, the boys hollered with excitement as they raced toward the wooden fort that was complete with tunnels and towers and slides.

"Hey, how come this table isn't buried in snow like the others?" I asked, sliding along the icy bench. I blew into my mittens to warm up my hands.

Eleanor didn't even look up from her secret sketchbook and box of colored pencils, which weren't a total secret, because I knew all about them. But she had never told her parents, particularly her mother, who expected Eleanor to spend all her free time on brainiac activities.

That's another person I didn't understand—Eleanor's mother. To be fair, I didn't actually know her; I only knew what Eleanor had told me. Besides, she was from another country, so she probably thought about the world in a very different way.

"I cleared it off so we could sit here," she said. "I ran down here as soon as we hung up."

I leaned over and studied her drawings. Wispy stick figures, standing at sharp angles and dressed in flowing clothes, covered the entire page. Eleanor bent her red pencil all around, scratching with the side of the pointy end, like she was adding cherry frosting.

"Those are so pretty."

"Thanks," she replied, the tip of her tongue sticking out of her mouth.

"And you could make real-life clothes from these pictures?"

"Yep. Especially if I had the Deluxe Electronic Pluckarama 1080."

"What's that?"

Eleanor sighed.

"The very best sewing and embroidery machine on the market."

I turned around and scanned the entire park as Eleanor finished her sketches. The sun was setting behind Sugar Mountain and the winds had died down. It was still early in the ski season, so I didn't see too many Outer ants gliding down the slopes. That's what everyone in town called the teeny-tiny people skiing way off in the distance—ants—like they were crawling all over the biggest, richest anthill ever.

I immediately slipped into daydreaming like I always do, this time imagining myself as one of those Outer ants, sliding down the snowy slope wearing a super-cute ski jacket and matching ski pants, then meeting JB and all my beautiful, fun friends at the lodge by the fireplace for hot chocolate with marshmallows and whipped cream, and one of Mim's mouthwatering Monster Chunk cookies that wasn't a broken leftover, but a whole, fresh cookie.

Just then, Henry ran over, wiggling and blowing into his bare hands.

"My fingers are falling off!"

"Well, what did you do with your mittens?"

"Stupid Charlie took them and lost them in a crack."

"Don't say *stupid*, Henry."

"Well, he is. Mean *and* stupid!"

Eleanor twisted around and dug into her backpack.

"Here," she said, handing Henry the cutest pair of yellow mittens I had ever seen, as soft as bunny fur. "They're a little big, but you can use these. They're extras."

"Those are too fancy for him," I said as Henry turned around and ran back to the swings.

"It's just yarn I found in a clearance bin. They were easy to knit."

"You *made* those?"

"Last January, when my mother had the flu. Since she was so sick, she didn't poke her head in my bedroom every five minutes, like she normally does. It gave me the chance to knit and crochet a few things. I have more; he can keep those."

"It doesn't make any sense," I said. "I don't get why your mother doesn't want you to do anything crafty. Mim would be thrilled if I made my own hats and scarves and blankets and whatever, so we didn't have to spend money on them."

Eleanor closed her sketchpad and slid it into her backpack.

"Because she wants me to be a rocket scientist or a neurosurgeon or—"

"Oops, you dropped something," I said, picking up a little folded pink piece of paper.

She grabbed it without saying anything.

"What is it?"

After folding it even smaller, Eleanor stuffed it into her pocket and mumbled, "Nothing important. So, what was I talking about?"

She seemed so flustered, I wondered if it was a note from school. Was it possible she had gotten in trouble?

"Umm, I think you were saying how your mother wants you to be a rock scientist."

"A rock-*et* scientist," she said. "Or she'd settle for a CFO or CEO, or possibly the leader of the Free World."

I was still baffled.

"Well, don't some of those people like to sew and knit?"

"Not where Amma comes from. Domestic arts are for women who have no education or careers. No bright futures."

"But what about all your chores you have to do at home?"

"That's separate. That's part of being in a family."

"Well, doing crafts and sketching pictures seems like a pretty strange thing to have to hide from your mother."

Eleanor smiled one of her giant stretchy grins that make her whole face light up.

"Looks like I won't have to hide it for a while. My father is generally very supportive and nonjudgmental, but he's never been the boss—until now."

"I almost forgot. How long is your mother going to be in New York?"

"Thaththa called from the airport. He said it depends on Nenda Soma's condition, as well as her level of care. Amma has gone to assess the situation, but Thaththa thinks she'll be away for at least two weeks."

I could tell Eleanor was wicked excited, but she also didn't want to say anything too disrespectful about her mother. I, on the other hand, would fall apart if Mim went anywhere for two weeks. She might work a lot and forget to clean the house and be tired all the time, but she was still the best stepmother in the whole world. She let us do almost anything, like stay up late, and she always made sure the cupboards were filled with lots of treats.

"Eleanor! A brilliant idea flash! Since our television is broken and you have two weeks off, do you want to meet here every day? This place can be our very own 'Dream Central' where we come up with plans to make our deepest dreams come true. Just like Madame M predicted. Plus, I can pretty much ignore the twins since they love the playground so much."

Eleanor tilted her head and gazed all around. The sun had disappeared behind Sugar Mountain, creating purple and blue streaks across the sky.

"Dream Central?" she grinned. "I like it."

JANUARY

A couple of weeks later, after I had rushed from school to pick up the twins, Mrs. Petite asked if I'd mind if the boys kept her company through dinner. Mr. Petite had his annual duck decoy potluck meeting, and she didn't want to eat alone.

If I'd mind?

Don't get me wrong, I love my little brothers, but it can be a pain watching them every day, particularly now since I had to get them organized for meetings with Eleanor down at Dream Central. For a split second, I considered keeping Mrs. Petite company, too—her whole house smelled of maple syrup pie, one of her specialties—but I was way too excited about my awesome find the night before.

For once, Mim hadn't gone directly to bed after supper, so we got a chance to chat. Right away, I asked if she knew anything about Pop's skiing days, and if they had skied together at Sugar Mountain.

"Oh my!" she cried, then burst out laughing. "I couldn't ski to save my life."

"Do you know if my mother skied?"

Mim took my hand and smiled.

"Yes, she did—at least, back when they were in high school. Your father told me they used to meet down at the lodge at the end of his shift, and they'd have a big cup of hot chocolate by the stone fireplace before hitting the slopes together."

"Really? Hot chocolate by the fireplace? That's so *romantic . . .*" I sighed.

"Wait! Do you mean Pop used to work at Sugar Mountain? What'd he do?"

"He was what they called a patroller. They would check on things, make sure no one was doing anything fishy or too flashy."

"Did Pop keep any of his old stuff?"

"Heavens, no. His equipment would be very outdated by now. Why are you so interested in your father's old skiing days?"

I hadn't been prepared for that question, and wasn't sure I wanted to tell Mim about my dreams, or about Madame M, and how I thought the Outer girls were all amazing. Normally, I told my stepmom pretty much everything, and she always answered any question I had . . . but this time I felt like I needed to keep things to myself for a while.

"Some kids at school joined the ski club, so I was just wondering."

"Well, we do have a pile of his old *Fresh Powder* magazines in our bedroom closet, if you know anyone who'd like those."

So, today, after leaving the boys with Mrs. Petite for the rest of the afternoon (and grabbing a licking icicle from her front porch), I was anxious to read the very first *Fresh Powder* in my father's collection, which I had fished out of the closet and tucked in my backpack the night before.

I was hurrying down Bon Hiver Lane, thinking about everything I had to tell Eleanor, when up ahead I saw that mysterious boy leaning against the inside of the tall black fence. He wore the same baggy green jacket down to his knees and a black hat that forced his messy dark curls over his glasses. A pair of binoculars hung from his neck, just like last time.

"Hey!" I said. "It's nice to finally meet you in person instead of talking through that box."

He stood up straight and fumbled with the binoculars like he was trying to think of something to spy on.

"Why are you hurrying?" he asked.

"Because you'd never believe the lucky day I'm having! Do you ever have days like that, when you can feel it in your bones?"

The boy crinkled his nose and tilted his head.

"Are you referring to a specific skeletal fracture?"

"Huh?" I replied.

This kid was starting to sound like Eleanor.

"What I mean is that *deep-down* feeling you get when something special is about to happen, and you're not sure where that special something is going to lead you, but everything keeps falling into place, so you're ready to jump on board and take the ride!"

He just stood there, his hands now shoved in his pockets, like he didn't know how to have a conversation. I noticed he was shivering a little. He probably wasn't used to the cold.

"So, are you ever going to tell me your name?" I asked.

I smiled extra wide as if his answer were the most important thing in the world, but he didn't smile back. He either had to be the shyest kid I'd ever met, or the rudest.

"In case you forgot, mine's Ruby LaRue. And if you want, you can come down to the playground with me and my friend, Eleanor. My little brothers are usually with me, too, so that's why we go to the playground, so they can play, but Eleanor and I mostly talk and make big plans and she sketches a lot, and today I brought a magazine."

He paused, then finally replied, "I don't have permission to leave the property."

It was strange hearing him say that behind the tall pointy fence, with that enormous mansion in the background. Somehow it looked more like a prison.

"Why not? Can't you just ask your parents if you want to go somewhere?"

He sneezed into the air, then pulled a tissue from his pocket and blew his nose. It took forever, like he was moving in slow motion. Then he turned around without answering and trudged through the snow, back toward his humongous home.

Even though I sorta felt sorry for him, I also felt a little annoyed with those strange silences of his, because, according to Mim, there are very few excuses in the world for being flat-out rude.

"Can't you even tell me your name?" I called out. "You know, it's not polite to not answer someone."

Still nothing. Just a slow march back to jail.

"Well, whoever you are, you can meet us anytime. Down at the playground on Winterberry Common, in the village. Also known as Dream Central. Where I'm gonna find my destiny. And Eleanor's gonna find hers too!"

But by the time I had said those last words he had opened a side door and disappeared . . . almost like his giant house had swallowed him up.

No matter how fast I hurried, Eleanor was always at the common first. The picnic table would be cleared of snow and she would be hard at work by the time I slid in next to her on the bench, drawing in her sketchbook or doing something crafty.

But today, I was surprised to see that she was nowhere in sight. It was strange not having the boys there either, and since no one ever played at the playground during the winter months, I was the only one in the park.

Snow had fallen overnight, as it did many nights in the mountains, so with the sleeve of my jacket, I brushed off our picnic table and sat down to wait.

At first it felt awkward and a little lonely sitting there all by myself, watching the cars and people hurry around the village, but then I began to let my mind drift, and I started to notice things. Like wind whistling through icy branches and frosty smells in the air. A lot of people complained about the winter, the cold and the dark, but I had decided it was my favorite time of year. I loved the way the snow made everything feel fresh and magical, like living inside a beautiful crystal snow globe.

That reminded me of Madame M, which reminded me of my prediction, which reminded me of skiing!

I pulled Pop's old *Fresh Powder* magazine from my backpack and turned to the table of contents. The main article with the biggest photo listed the best mountains out west. I didn't care about that, since who knows if I'll ever get the chance to visit a fancy place like Aspen or Jackson Hole. The second one showed you how to wax cross-country skis—nope, not interested in moving *up* a hill of snow. But the third story, titled "Getting in Ultimate Shape for the Ultimate Skier," was exactly what I had been looking for—somewhere to start.

I flipped directly to that article because I knew skiing probably used different muscles than the ones I had been using all my life. I stood up and placed the magazine on the table in front of me and mimicked the lady in the photo (who looked like an Outer) by trying to get my right foot up onto the table, but it was too high, so I dropped my foot onto the bench instead.

Then I was supposed to bend my left knee while clasping my hands behind my back and lean everything forward over my right leg to stretch three different muscles I couldn't pronounce. I couldn't do that stretch, either. I mean, you practically had to be a gymnast to twist your body like that.

When I tried to yank my right foot off the bench, my boot got caught and I fell back into a drift of snow.

"What are you doing?"

Eleanor was looking down at me.

"I'm working out!"

She offered her hand and helped me up.

"*You're* working out?"

"Look! My father has tons of these at home," I said, pointing to the magazine. "Everything I need to know about skiing, so I can be in tiptop shape for my lesson at Sugar Mountain."

"Wow, that's great, Ruby."

But I couldn't tell if she really meant it, because she dropped her backpack onto the table like it weighed a thousand pounds and then slumped down onto the bench.

"What's wrong? Oh, no. Has your mother come home already? Is that why you're late?"

"No, it's not that."

Eleanor's amma was still taking care of her sick aunt, Nenda Soma, in New York, which meant Eleanor continued to do almost anything she wanted to do, with her father's full support. Eleanor said her thaththa had been so quiet all these years that she had no idea he even disagreed with her mother's strict, controlling ways. But now he practically pushed her out the door, canceling all her lessons and clubs and extra advanced classes—at least while her mother was gone—so Eleanor could hang out and do as she pleased.

So every afternoon, even if a snowstorm blew through, we met at Dream Central to talk about our favorite things. Sometimes we "brainstormed" (one of Eleanor's words), which meant we helped each other come up with ways to make our dream predictions come true. So far we were stuck on the moneymaking part, which was a problem, since that was exactly what we needed in order to get going.

But other times, we chatted about stuff like the popular girls at school, and what made them so popular, and the meanest teachers and what made them so mean, and wicked cute boys, like JB Knox, except I didn't bring him up too often, because Eleanor always acted weird when I talked about my huge crush on him. I think she still thought of boys as disgusting show-offs who barged into everyone, took the best seats in class, and sometimes said awful things. Which basically described Anton Orlov from the Math Squad, who was obviously in love with Eleanor, but showed it by acting like a jerk.

JB was nothing like that. He glided through the hallways smiling at everyone he passed, the dreamiest dreamboat in all of Paris.

"Amma's still in New York," said Eleanor, using a pen to scrape at a mound of ice on the picnic table. "Thaththa said she'll most likely stay for many more weeks."

"But that's good, right? Or do you miss her now?"

"No, I'm not missing her." She sighed loudly. "Perhaps, her cooking. Amma cooks much better than Thaththa. But that's not it. Well, and the way she does the laundry. She scents it with lavender water and folds the clothes precisely, but at least I don't have to iron. No, really, I'm fine with her gone for a while. More than fine."

"Then what's wrong? I'm having one of the *luckiest* days of my life, and can feel my destiny about to explode! But I can't enjoy it if you're upset, Eleanor."

"I wouldn't say I'm upset; just a little disappointed. But you shouldn't allow my demeanor to affect your disposition, Ruby."

Eleanor and her giant words.

"I don't know what any of that means, but, Eleanor—I can't be happy if you aren't happy. So what is it? Why are you disappointed?"

She took a deep breath and said, "My father said, '*Absolutely not.*'"

"To what?"

"Changing his mind and giving me a job at his gas station. He said going to school and studying was my job. That there'll be plenty of time for me to make money when I'm an adult."

"Oh, is that all?" I replied, and smiled. "Don't worry, we'll think of something else."

"Like what, Ruby? Robbing a bank? How will we ever earn the money to fulfill our destinies?"

"You *have* to try and be more glass half-full, Eleanor. I *know* our predictions will come true. We just haven't figured out all the steps to make it happen yet."

Eleanor sighed. "I wish we could consult Madame Magnifique."

"I know. It's so strange how she's disappeared."

Every chance we got now, we checked for signs of Madame M, but she was nowhere to be found. Just like Eleanor had told me on the phone, the whole alley was off limits, with Dumpsters blocking the entrance, plus the poster in Wonderland's was missing, and so was the Apparition Way street sign. But the really baffling thing was that no one else had ever heard of her. It was as if she had never been there—as if she had been part of a dream.

Eleanor sighed again and then glanced around the playground.

"Where're your brothers?"

"Mrs. Petite asked if they could stay with her through dinner, so that's one of the reasons I'm feeling extra lucky, because we can do anything we want to do without worrying about the boys ruining stuff. But I'm getting super hungry . . . Mrs. Petite was baking her famous maple syrup pie, and I can't get that smell out of my head."

"I'm a little hungry, too," said Eleanor.

"You are?"

That surprised me, since Eleanor never seems to get hungry, and hardly eats anything when she does eat. She picks at her food and takes tiny bites, which makes me even hungrier to watch.

"Hey! Do you want to walk over to my house? You've never been, and we can eat some of yesterday's Monster Chunk cookies, the ones Mim brings home from the café!"

"Okay," she said, and jumped up like she was feeling better already. "It is unusual we've never visited each other's homes."

Which was exactly what I wanted her to say, because from everything Eleanor had told me about her life all these years, I couldn't wait to visit her home next. I mean, how could we have been best friends all this time and never even seen each other's houses?

This really *was* turning out to be one of the luckiest days of my life.

At the far end of Maine Street we turned left at Bon Hiver Lane, where I hoped we would get a chance to see that strange boy through his tall black fence.

"I told him about Dream Central, and that he should come and hang out with us if he wants. But to tell you the truth, I can't figure out what the deal is with him. He's kind of rude. He won't even tell me his name."

Eleanor shrugged her shoulders and said, "Maybe he doesn't know how friendship works."

"What? How is that possible?"

"Socially challenged individuals aren't always able to appropriately bond with others."

"I don't know what that means, Eleanor, but you're thinking about it way too hard. Being friends with someone is simple."

"Not for everyone."

Sometimes I can't figure out where Eleanor gets her ideas; I mean, making a friend is like breathing air or falling asleep—something that just happens without thinking about it.

A few minutes later we turned into my long driveway, a winter paradise winding through tall pine trees laced with ice.

"Ta-*dah!*" I cried as our old blue house came into sight. "I can't believe you've never been here before. Home sweet home."

The cat hobbled toward us from underneath the far end of our porch and rubbed up against our legs.

"That's Marilyn," I told Eleanor. "Mim named her after Marilyn Monroe, because she used to be so glamorous and beautiful, like the real Marilyn Monroe, but that was a long time ago, before Mim married my dad."

As soon as we entered the front door, I could smell last night's dinner—fried clams from Cap'n Smitty's Clam Shack—so now I was really hungry. The empty cardboard box was still wide open on the kitchen table.

"Hey, Eleanor! I forgot to tell you, our TV is fixed. Do you wanna watch *The Price Is Right*? It's the old version with Bob Barker, which Mim watched when she was our age. It's much better than the one on now, with what's-his-name."

Eleanor kicked off her boots and shrugged her shoulders. "Whatever."

I got the bag of yesterday's leftover Monster Chunk pieces out of the fridge.

"Do you like your cookies microwaved? They get all melty, like they just came out of the oven."

"Sure," said Eleanor, but she didn't seem to be listening because she was staring all around our house.

After heating the cookie chunks in the bag I dumped them on the coffee table to see which kinds were left. Eleanor had neatly stacked all the twins' toys at one end of the sofa so we could sit down.

"Looks like peanut butter cream, snickerdoodle, and a couple of triple fudge pieces," I announced, studying the pile with my expert eye.

"Interesting choices," said Eleanor, as she sat on the very edge of the couch and squinted at them.

"What do you want to drink?" I asked. "We've got cola, root beer, orangeade, and—"

"Water is fine."

"Water? That's not a drink. That's something you use to rinse your teeth after brushing. Don't you want a real drink, like soda?"

"I like water."

I got up and searched for a clean glass in the cabinet, but all of them were used and sitting by the sink. So I grabbed a Wicked Big Gulp plastic cup and filled it to the top and got a can of root beer for myself out of the fridge.

As I handed the water to Eleanor, I suddenly felt really excited inside. I was so happy to have her over to my house!

But I noticed Eleanor had a confused expression on her face, and she wasn't even watching the television or eating the cookies, because she was still studying everything like she was in a foreign country.

I was about to ask her if she had an upset stomach or something when she said the strangest thing to me.

"Ruby? Why don't you clean up?"

I took a swig of soda and wiped my mouth.

"Huh?"

"If your father is away a lot and your stepmother works all the time and comes home tired, why don't you help?"

That was something I had never even thought of before . . . Mim was the one who was supposed to do that kind of stuff.

" 'Cause I'm watching the boys, silly—remember?"

"But you said they do nothing but stare at the TV when you're home."

I didn't know what this had to do with anything.

"First of all, and no offense, Eleanor, my stepmother isn't uptight like your amma. She lets us have fun the way it's supposed to be when you're a kid. And second of all, not everyone is in love with cleaning and organizing like you—not that there's anything wrong with that, but still, it makes it easier to relax."

Eleanor sat quietly with her face scrunched like she was trying to figure out what I was talking about. I continued to watch *The Price Is Right* and picked through the pile of cookies all on my own, since Eleanor didn't seem that hungry after all. They were playing one of my favorite games (the one where Bob Barker asks the contestant to arrange five numbers to guess the correct price of a brand-new automobile) when I heard a bang.

"Sorry!" came Eleanor's voice from the kitchen.

I walked over and peered over the counter just as she scooped up a bunch of packages from the floor.

"Oh, don't worry about that. Boxes fall out of the cabinets all the time. Are you looking for something else to eat?"

She didn't say anything as she tried to shove the cartons back inside. Then she opened the cupboard next to it and stared.

Mim kept our kitchen well stocked, so we had almost every delicious snack you could think of. I was pretty sure Eleanor's mother never let her have anything fun to eat.

"I know, it's hard to pick," I said as I walked around and stood next to her, "but you can have anything you want."

I grabbed a Caramel Crunchy from the middle shelf, unwrapped it, and took a bite.

"*Mountains of sugar . . .*" Eleanor mumbled under her breath.

"Mountains of Sugar?" I asked Eleanor. "Never heard of that one. What's in it? Toffee, chocolate, peanuts?"

Eleanor took a deep breath and then blew out a long puff of air like she was blowing up a balloon.

"Do you eat this every day, Ruby?"

"Eat what?" I asked between bites.

"All of this?"

She made little circles in the air in front of the shelves.

I paused a second and swallowed.

"Do you mean *food?*"

Eleanor frowned at me like I had given the wrong answer at the exact same time Bob Barker told the woman on TV that she hadn't won the automobile, and the "too bad" music came on.

"Oh, *too bad*, Doris, but thanks for playing!" said Bob.

And that's when Eleanor really lost her mind.

As if it weren't strange enough that she didn't recognize food when she saw it, out of the blue, Eleanor tiptoed over to the television, clicked it off during a commercial for diapers, and said, "Let's clean."

I couldn't figure out what had gotten into her.

"Excuse me?" I said.

"Housework goes faster when you do it with another person."

"But Eleanor, I wanna do something *fun*. You've never been to my house before, and we've been suffering in school all day."

"Cleaning is the sort of activity that isn't fun until the end. The results are the reward."

What was she talking about? I was beginning to think her mother had brainwashed her.

"Eleanor, I don't think you understand that some people—or, probably, most people, or at least most *normal* people, like me—just aren't cut out to be fussy neatniks like you!"

Eleanor put on her serious face.

"Ruby. What if I promised you that getting organized would help you achieve your dreams?"

This sounded like a trick to me.

"Which dream?"

"Every dream you've ever had," she replied. "Even your dream of becoming an Outer."

That's when one of those idea-lights went off in my brain, telling me to listen to Eleanor. Because even though I saw no connection between becoming an Outer and cleaning the house—and I hated cleaning more than just about anything—Eleanor was basically successful at everything she ever touched, and more talented than anyone I knew.

We started with the kitchen, since we were already there, and I had to admit, it was pretty messy. We wiped down the cabinets and counters and appliances, which ended up smelling as good as they looked, not sticky like they usually were. After loading the dishwasher and pressing the button, she washed and dried the extra dishes piled in the sink, while I swept the floor around Marilyn, who seemed annoyed by all the commotion.

"Done in exactly twenty-six minutes," said Eleanor. "Next, we'll do that area by the couch."

"The family room, too? I think the kitchen is enough. Besides, you don't want my stepmom to die of shock when she walks through the door."

All this work made me tired, so I grabbed another Caramel Crunchy from the cupboard.

"It will only take a few more minutes, Ruby."

Eleanor isn't a bossy person, but when she gets something in her head, it's practically impossible to stop her from finishing. So while Eleanor sorted piles of old newspapers and catalogs to recycle, I gathered up Charlie's and Henry's action figures and all the matching parts, like the tiny ninja swords and miniature ninja shields. As I dug around in one of our built-in storage drawers looking for an extra plastic container, Eleanor leaned in behind me.

Her eyes popped out of her head.

"What?" I asked.

"That!" she said.

"Which *that?* What are you looking at?"

"Do I see yarn? And knitting needles?"

"Oh, that's Mim's old stuff. She used to knit a lot and do crafts when I was young, before the boys were born and she only worked part—"

Eleanor cut me off. "And you never told me?"

"Never told you what?"

"That your stepmother likes to *knit?*"

"I don't know, I guess I forgot because she doesn't do it anymore. She doesn't have time."

Well, you would have thought I'd cracked open a carton of brand-new books. Eleanor's wide brown eyes practically sprang out of her head as she pawed through the drawer.

"How much?!" she asked, turning over a wad of blue yarn, squishing it between her fingers.

"I have no idea how much she has, because there's a ton more in the hall closet, and maybe—"

Eleanor covered my mouth.

"Money," she said. "How much *money* to buy it all? I have a little left over from my birthday last year."

"Oh, you don't have to pay for it. Mim has been meaning to call the art teacher at the elementary school to donate it because she didn't want to see it go to waste. I swear, you can have it all if you want."

At first, Eleanor frowned like she didn't believe me. Then slowly her mouth rolled out one of her special ribbon smiles until her face stretched as wide as it could go.

"Just to be sure it's okay, you have to ask your stepmother, Ruby. And if she says yes, I promise I will make something very nice for her in return."

"Really? Like what?"

Eleanor shrugged. "Anything. A hat, mittens, placemats."

And that's when *the best idea I ever had* hit me, like a shooting star falling from way up in the sky! But more like a shooting star that streaks by and then disappears behind the mountains, because we couldn't have possibly imagined where my idea would end up landing.

"I can't believe we didn't think of this before, Eleanor; like, it's *so* obvious. This is *too* exciting!!"

"I know. And it's not like it's a real job or anything, so technically I'm not going behind Thaththa's back, even though I don't think I should tell him . . . not yet, anyway."

"We can finally make some money! What've we got so far?"

Eleanor took notes since she has that pretty, swoopy kind of handwriting—mine is so sloppy that half the time I can't even read it.

"Okay, our company is called E and R Dream Designs, which is the abbreviation for Eleanor and Ruby, and the *dream* part is obvious." Eleanor stopped herself and asked, "Are you sure it shouldn't be R and E Dream Designs?"

"Of course not. You're the one making our *gorgeous* creations. I'm just selling them. Anyone with a little extra friendliness can do that."

"But this was all your idea, and I couldn't make them without your stepmother's supplies."

"Believe me, you're doing Mim a favor by clearing out all this junk. She complains about it all the time. So keep reading. What's next?"

Eleanor looked back at the notes in her lap and read aloud:

"ONE: Eleanor creates wicked cool stuff from Mim's leftover yarn and craft supplies.

TWO: Ruby is the awesome salesperson who will try to convince lots of stores in the village to carry Eleanor's wicked cool stuff.

THREE: Eleanor and Ruby split their profits equally.

FOUR: Ruby will spend the money she makes on ski lessons with a cute ski instructor so she can meet amazing Outers and become one of them and go to the annual Snow Ball (hopefully with JB Knox) and be forever happy.

FIVE: Eleanor will save her money to purchase a Deluxe Electronic Pluckarama 1080 Sew-Good and Embroidery Machine, and someday develop a line of haute couture which will be worn by people from Paris, New Hampshire, to Paris, France."

Eleanor stopped reading.

"I'm not too comfortable with the embellishments," she said.

"The *what-a-ments?*"

Eleanor leaned forward and spoke slowly as if that would help me understand her huge words better.

"Don't you feel we're jinxing ourselves by adding superlatives and projecting unrealistic outcomes?" she asked. "I mean, it should be a basic business plan with a straightforward contractual agreement."

I took a long sip from my third can of soda and thought for a second. Sometimes it was hard to explain to Eleanor how real life worked.

"I think the problem is, you're complicating everything. Why don't you knit a few adorable thingies and I'll try to get a store to display them and we'll see how it goes. Okay?"

Right then, the front door swung open and banged against the wall.

"*Mim!* You're early!" I said. "Oh, Eleanor, you get to meet Mim, and Mim, you get to meet Eleanor."

My stepmom dropped her bags on the kitchen table and stretched out her arms.

"Eleanor! I'm so happy to finally meet you."

Eleanor had a funny look on her face like she was in trouble. She backed away a little and asked, "Do you need help with your groceries, Mrs. LaRue?"

"I need nothing but a big old welcome hug!"

Eleanor stiffened up like she had never hugged anyone in her life; her arms were boards along her sides, and she squeezed her eyes shut as my stepmother squished her tight.

"MIM! Look around! We cleaned!!"

"You did?" she asked, as she transferred her arms over to me. "Well, would you look at that! How wonderful! Thank you, girls. Now, are you two interested in some dinner? I didn't get as much take-out since the boys are eating over at the Petites' house, but I can always dig up something in the freezer to microwave."

"Thank you, but . . . umm," Eleanor stammered, "I didn't realize it was so late. I should go."

Then she bent down to the floor and began stuffing the yarn back into the drawers.

"What are you doing, Eleanor? Don't you want to take all that home so you can start knitting?"

She shook her head hard, like she was embarrassed.

"Wait a second," I said. "Mim? Can we give Eleanor your old yarn and stuff to knit things? She's practically an expert like you used to be, and we're starting a business to sell her crafts so we can make some money. Plus, she's the reason we cleaned up the house."

"A business to make money?" Mim asked, looking very impressed. "Please, take it all, Eleanor. You'd be doing me a favor, getting rid of all that junk."

Eleanor managed to unfreeze and stood up.

"At least take it in appreciation for doing such a nice job tidying up around here," Mim added, as she emptied a grocery bag, stuffed the yarn into it, and handed it to Eleanor. I could tell Eleanor didn't know what to say, but she smiled and took the bag.

"Thank you."

"No, thank *you*," said Mim. "And don't you ever forget—our door is always open. *Tu es ici chez toi.*"

"That's French," I told Eleanor. "It basically means, *Our house is your house.* Right, Mim?"

"*Très bien, ma chérie!*"

As Eleanor slipped on her jacket, a note dropped out of her pocket. I picked it up. "What's this?"

"A list," she said quickly, before yanking it from my hand. "A few things my father asked me to pick up."

"Geez, Eleanor. You'd think it was top-secret information."

But instead of laughing, Eleanor thanked Mim one last time, then raced out the front door and down the driveway with that bag of yarn like it was stolen merchandise.

It turns out the timing could not have been better to start our business, because it was that boring period in January when everyone was burned out from the same old fashions and trends and holiday clearance sales. The store owners seemed even happier that our "collection" was locally made, because that made our stuff "quaint," or some word like that. Also, Eleanor (who is full of cute little artsy ideas) came up with an adorable label that she attached to everything, which says E & R DREAM DESIGNS OF PARIS, NEW HAMPSHIRE, like we are a real fancy specialty company.

So, selling Eleanor's stuff was a cinch. The problem was, we quickly sold out of everything she had already created, and our customers demanded more ASAP! That's when my next idea-light went off, which was a good thing, since I knew I couldn't help Eleanor knit (I mean, I can barely lace up my snow boots), but at least I had what Eleanor called "natural marketing acumen," which she told me was the same as having good business sense.

We were back at Dream Central one afternoon, brainstorming. In reality, that meant I daydreamed, while Eleanor sketched and the boys played.

"I've been thinking, Eleanor. What if you made smaller items, like key chains and bracelets and bookmarks?"

It was the third week in January, and we were spending a lot less time at Dream Central these days because I was busy with customers in the village and Eleanor was busy manufacturing at home (while her thaththa worked at the gas station). But most days, we still met for a few minutes at the playground to give each other what Eleanor called "daily updates," and so that I could work out, following the exercises in my father's *Fresh Powder* magazines. And of course, the twins burned off the sillies, running around and playing.

"Ruby," said Eleanor, "that's your best idea yet! I've been up late every night in my bedroom, trying to knit pieces in one day that normally take a week. My fingers are aching. It's so obvious! Why didn't we think of that before?"

"It came to me when I pitched E and R Dream Designs to Mrs. Wilder, the owner of the Treasure Chest. You know how they have all sorts of little trinkets in there? I thought to myself over and over, can Eleanor *knit* that? I even thought about cat collars and table coasters."

I hated thinking of Eleanor working so hard every night, but so far we had each made only $65.47. Don't get me wrong; neither of us had ever had that kind of money before, but I quickly realized we'd need to make a lot more, a lot faster, in time for everything to fall into place for my magical evening at the Snow Ball with the one and only JB Knox. The big night was just a little more than two months away.

"I had another idea, too. You could use my stepmother's old scrapbook supplies and knit them into jewelry or whatever. She pulled out another box from the back of the closet yesterday, and it was full of cute knickknacks like antique buttons and charms and polished stones with holes through the middle. She said we could have all of it."

This time, Eleanor squealed.

"Can you bring the box to school with you tomorrow?" she asked. "I'll start right away and work through the weekend."

"Is tomorrow Friday already?" I leaned over and stretched my legs. "I can't believe how time flies now. It's like I'm falling back into bed as soon as I get up."

Just then, Henry ran over and asked if he could talk to a big kid he saw standing behind a bush.

"What big kid?"

I twisted around to where he pointed, but all I saw was frozen trees, crackling as the wind pushed them up against one another.

"I guess he's gone," said Henry.

"Do you know his name?"

"Nope."

"What did he look like?"

"Tall and skinny."

Eleanor asked, "Did you notice what he was wearing?"

"A big green jacket and a black hat."

"I can't believe it," I said. "It sounds just like that new boy I was telling you about."

I had stopped searching for that kid behind his iron jail fence since nowadays I was always in a rush. First, I had to fetch the twins at the Petites', then hurry them down to Dream Central to quickly wear them out, and meet with Eleanor, then race into town to sell our designs, dragging the boys with me, all before it got dark.

"How many times have you seen him, Henry?"

"I don't know. A bunch. He hides behind the fort," he said. Then Henry whined, "I'm *staaarrrving*."

Since we were always running here and there, the boys and I had been skipping our afternoon snack. But I hadn't been missing it, which was strange, because I used to be hungry practically all the time.

"I have a banana," said Eleanor, "and some leftover spiced nuts and date bread."

"It's hard to believe that kid's been spying on us," I said. "I wonder if he's been coming over here for weeks, or what? He's obviously shy or something, even though I told him it's okay to hang out with us. He doesn't have to sneak around. I mean, it's not like we're gonna bite his head off or anything."

"Can I have the banana?" Henry asked Eleanor as Charlie ran over.

"You two can have it all," she replied, passing her snacks to both of the boys.

"I'm thirsty," said Charlie. "Do you have any root beer?"

"Don't be rude," I said. "She's not a refrigerator."

"I don't mind," said Eleanor, digging through her backpack. "No soda, though, which isn't a drink technically—more like pouring sugar down your throat. But I do have some extra water bottles."

"Oh, they aren't gonna drink . . ."

But before I could finish my sentence Charlie grabbed the water and followed Henry back to the fort.

"Ruby, stand up and take off your hat," said Eleanor.

"My hat? Why?"

"To measure your head. Your brilliant strategy gave me an idea for a headband."

As I stood, my pants stuck to the bench, which happens sometimes when the ice warms against the material. But when I yanked them up, they fell down again.

"I need new clothes," I said as Eleanor removed my E & R Dream Designs winter cap. "It's weird; everything I own is loose."

Eleanor had a piece of yarn in her pocket, which she wrapped around my head, then tied a small knot in it to mark the size.

"It's not weird," she said. "You're outside a lot more now, and you're doing those ski exercises from the magazine."

"You think that's it?"

"You're also not wheezing as much either, Ruby."

She was right. I had noticed that, ever since my psychic reading, my life had definitely changed for the better, and I had gotten a lot busier. But until now, I hadn't noticed that my body was changing too.

Eleanor pulled a few other things from her pocket, including a piece of paper the color of a detention note. She stuffed it right back in her jacket.

"*Ohmygosh*, were *you* tardy for school?" I asked.

"No," she said, but she refused to look at me, so I knew she was embarrassed by something. "I was just looking for a pen and paper to write down your knitting ideas, but I can remember it all."

"Eleanor," I said, "you can tell me stuff like that, you know. It's not like I haven't had my share of warning notices. Remember, it's not good to try to be Miss Perfect all the time. Plus, I can give you tons of advice when it comes to dealing with Mr. Tankhorn. Or anyone else, for that matter."

"Thanks, Ruby," she said. "It's nothing."

The next day, Eleanor and I sat down to lunch in the school cafeteria, sharing a table like we always do with her brainiac friends, those boys from the Math Squad who practically drool all over her even though she's completely clueless in that department.

Eleanor is the kind of girl who could be super pretty if she wanted to be, but has no idea of her potential—like, she doesn't even check the mirror and wonder about a new hairstyle, or whether she should wear lip gloss or anything like that. And honestly, it seems really strange to me that her passion in life is to launch a fashion line, because clothes seem to be the last thing on her mind.

Today, for example, she was wearing a plain yellow shirt and blue corduroys, which I have to admit isn't totally her fault, because her mother doesn't allow her to buy jeans or leggings. But at least she's not making her wear skirts and jumpers anymore, like she had to every day all the way through the end of fourth grade.

"Eleanor! You will never believe what happened last night after I asked Mim for her box of crafty things!" I said.

"Oooooh—let *me* guess!" yelled Anton Orlov, the loud, obnoxious captain of the Math Squad. "You sat on the box and it broke?"

His four brainiac friends burst out laughing like they did every time Anton said anything.

I don't know why we ever sit with them, except Eleanor claims it helps them to unite as a team. But lately she's taken a break from Math Squad since her thaththa told her to (and also to secretly keep up with all her knitting orders), so you'd think we could sit somewhere else for a change.

"*Hilarious*, Anton," I snapped back. "For your information, this has nothing to do with you, so you can go ahead and keep arguing about word problems and Rubik's Cubes and all the other boring subjects that fascinate your oversized brain."

"Just tell me what happened," said Eleanor.

I leaned into her shoulder and whispered, "Mim told me she can get *two free tickets* to the—*SB!*"

"The Snow Ball?"

"Yep! She found even more boxes of pretty trinkets and trimmings for you to make stuff, and then asked what we were going to do with all the money we've been earning with E and R. For a second I felt bad, because I thought maybe she assumed I was going to help her buy the Aqua-Pedic aboveground pool, or at least contribute to the family income so Pop could take a break from all his road trips. But then I told her that you wanted a fancy high-tech sewing machine, which she thought was an awesome idea. And then I confessed *I* was saving my money mostly to buy tickets to go to the Snow Ball, because I didn't want to tell her about the skiing part."

"So what did she say?"

"At first, she looked at me all funny, like I'd just announced I wanted to fly to the moon or something, and then she said, 'Well, I can get you *free* tickets to *that*.' I almost fainted, Eleanor!"

Eleanor looked at me a little funny, too.

"She actually said they're *free?*"

"All the Sugar Mountain employees get to go if they want, along with a date, but Mim said she didn't know any employees who ever went, and said that she wouldn't go even if they paid her, because she had no interest in partying with her customers. And she definitely knew Pop wouldn't want to go even if they were serving pot roast and waffle fries, which is his favorite dinner."

Eleanor squeezed her left eye shut, the way she did when she was thinking extra hard about something.

"So what did she say about *you* wanting to go?"

But right at that exact moment my mind went blank, because out of 172 Paris Middle School kids, the one and only JB Knox was walking directly toward me.

"Hey, it's the gym girls," he said, and stopped in front of our table.

I couldn't believe it. He was talking to me! Again!

I felt my mouth drop wide open as JB took a swig of blue Gatorade and shook his head to get his curly hair out of his face, which was about the cutest thing in the world.

"Hi, JB," I managed to squeak. "How's ski club?"

"Awesome," he said, and knocked the table twice with his knuckles. "Turns out some of the Outers are really cool. I've been hanging with a bunch of them at the mountain."

JB was friends with Outers?

I had so many questions, especially since I had only two months left to ask him out to the Snow Ball. But before I could say another word, annoying Anton butted in.

"No seventh graders allowed on this side," he announced. "Sixth-grade section only."

What was he thinking?

I glared at Anton with more anger than I'd ever felt in my entire life, but Eleanor just stared down at her food and poked it with a fork.

"Big man!" said JB as he laughed and walked back into the crowd. "Later, kids."

"*Anton!*" I yelled. "What is wrong with you? Do you know who that is?"

"Yep. The biggest doofus in the school," he replied, which made the Squad boys giggle.

"No, that would be *you,*" I growled.

"Forget it, Ruby," said Eleanor. I know she hates it when anyone argues. "You didn't finish your story?"

"Yeah, Ruby, finish your boring story!" Anton snapped.

Boys like Anton were a complete mystery to me. Why would they think that acting obnoxious was the way to impress girls? Why couldn't they all be just like JB?

"Ignore him," mumbled Eleanor. "So tell me, what did your stepmother say?"

"*Arrgghh,*" I groaned. "I can't remember. Where was I?"

"The free tickets?" she whispered.

"Oh yeah. Well, even though Mim has zero interest in the Snow Ball, she said she could see why a fancy dance like that would appeal to someone my age."

"Really?" she asked. "Wow, your stepmom is *so* nice."

To be honest, Mim added a lot more words and descriptions that weren't exactly "nice" and shocked me a little, since she's usually the sweetest person in the room. But Mim said it's maddening to think about rich people spending more money on their designer gowns than she makes in a six-day week baking Monster Chunk cookies ten hours a day from her own secret recipe.

"So now that you know you can go, and you don't have to purchase the tickets, what do you plan to do with your earnings?"

"I'm not sure, but I think I want to start ski lessons a lot sooner now, and maybe take more than one or two, so I can get really good," I replied too loudly.

"Ski lessons!" Anton hollered. "Have you ever even been on skis, LaRue?"

"Why would I need ski lessons if I've already skied, Anton?"

"Have *you* ever been on skis?" Eleanor asked.

"I hate skiing," he said, dodging the question, which was so typical of a kid like him who twists everything around to make himself seem better than everyone else. "Who wants to hang around with a bunch of snobby Outers from nowheresville?"

"You wouldn't say that if you were one of them," I snapped back, "because then you would be the happiest kid on earth."

Anton stood up and shouted, "HA! I already *am* the happiest kid on earth."

Then the rest of the brainiacs stood up, too, and followed their leader to the garbage cans to dump their trays.

"Don't let him bother you," said Eleanor. "Believe me, he'll argue anything. He's actually not that bad once you get to know him."

Just then, I noticed Anton stop to pick up something from the floor. It looked like a headset. He gave it to Lewis, a hearing-impaired boy in our grade. Lewis smiled and Anton high-fived him.

For a brief second, I wondered if I could actually be wrong about Anton.

FEBRUARY

"How about five o'clock?" Eleanor asked. "You should walk over before it gets dark."

I had almost keeled over when I got the call from Eleanor this morning. Saturday is my day to sleep in, of course, since my alarm rings before dawn during the week. So I knew something had to be up when the phone rang extra early, which almost never happens on the weekend.

Mim had already left for work, and the twins were still in bed, too, so at first I thought it might be an emergency, like Pop calling from the road. When it turned out to be Eleanor, sounding super cheerful, it was just about the best way to wake up on a Saturday, especially when she said she was calling to invite me to dinner.

I would have canceled plans with the Head Outer (if there were one) to get a dinner invite to Eleanor's house. It's not like I haven't been hinting forever. She said it was her father's idea—that he really wanted to get to know Eleanor's friends, starting with me, her *best* friend!

To be sure it was okay, I called Mim at the Slope Side Café. She was just as excited as I was, and even offered to buy a gift box of assorted Monster Chunk cookies with her employee discount for me to take along as a present, which is the polite thing to do when you're invited to someone's house for a meal.

After making all our plans, I was so wound up with excitement, I didn't know what I would do with myself for the rest of the day as I waited for dinnertime to roll around. It was snowing hard outside, practically a blizzard, so I didn't feel like dragging the twins down to the playground or looping through town to check on customers in this weather. And I knew Eleanor would be busy right up until supper, making cute rainbow chokers, since we had recently received a rush order for them from the Treasure Chest.

The twins were happily lounging on the couch, watching cartoons, eating bowls of Honey-Os cereal, but I just couldn't stop fidgeting. I thought and thought about what I should do as I scanned the room—and that's when it hit me. I decided to clean! I don't know why, because I'm not an uptight neatnik in any way, but I hoped it might lead to something else, like it had with Eleanor and me; plus, I had to admit that it did feel good to see the results.

So I started with sweeping the floors, which were all wood except in our bedrooms, where we have carpeting, and right away it looked like my cleaning had led to something else. The broom picked up a folded piece of paper from underneath the couch, exactly like one of those little pieces of paper Eleanor had been stuffing in her pockets lately.

At first, I wasn't sure if I should open it, but decided I had to, in case it was important:

WEAR A YELLOW SHIRT IF YES. WEAR A RED SHIRT IF NO.

It was signed only with the letters "NA" at the bottom.

I figured it was probably something Pop had written down before a road trip, although it didn't make much sense. Who knew how long it could have been tucked under the sofa? Pop hadn't been home since his short break during the holidays. So I decided to toss the note, and continued cleaning and sorting like crazy until the snowstorm had passed.

The family room and kitchen were as "neat as a pin," according to Mim, who arrived just before it was time for me to leave for Eleanor's house. Mim said it made her feel almost as good as having Pop home, which suddenly made me miss him more than usual. He had never been away this long before, but I didn't say anything—I didn't want to spoil Mim's happy mood.

The sun had already begun to set behind the mountains as I walked down our driveway, even though the whole world still felt fresh and crisp and sparkling clean. I was so excited to visit Eleanor's house for the first time that I rushed over without checking the mystery boy's giant yard to see if he was around, and to ask why he had been spying on us. I even forgot to peek behind the Dumpsters down Apparition Way for signs of Madame M as I power-walked through the village.

Since I'd hurried over to Eleanor's so fast, I arrived fifteen minutes early, which seemed too soon to land at someone's house as a guest, so I set down my cookie gift box on their front steps and spelled out a snow message in the Bandaranaikes' side yard that said THANK YOU!!

Their house was one level and painted a creamy yellow. It looked brand-new. I checked my watch, picked up the cookie box, and rang the doorbell at exactly five o'clock.

When Eleanor cracked the door open I could barely contain my excitement.

"MIM SENT OVER A DOZEN NON-REJECT MONSTER CHUNK COOKIES IN ONE OF THE SPECIAL SLOPE SIDE CAFÉ CARTONS FOR DESSERT!!" I shouted, before the door was fully opened.

She stared, almost as if she didn't recognize me.

"Welcome, Ruby!" said Mr. B, who appeared at Eleanor's side. "We're delighted to have you join us."

"Hi there, Mr. B! Thanks for having me," I said, plowing through the front door. "Wow! I just love your house."

"Thank you," he said, smiling hard. "Please make yourself at home."

"Ruby," Eleanor whispered as she caught my arm, "you have to take off your boots."

I glanced down and saw that both Eleanor and her father were wearing thin foreign sandals.

"Oh, this is going to be *so* fun. Everything's already wicked different."

I gave them tons of compliments on their decorations, which is the thing to do when you go to someone's home for the first time, but in this case I totally meant everything I said, because their house was super cute and neat and reminded me of a dollhouse.

"Oooooh, that's a nice vase . . . and I love this gold rug! That picture of elephants doesn't look like anything you'd buy here in Paris."

"This way, Ruby," said her father, so I followed him, in stocking feet, down the bright hallway to the family room.

"And you have so many windows—but I know that's because we live in a really old house, and in the olden days they didn't have so many windows, to keep the heat in, except they usually had a couple windows in the front of the house, like ours, so you could see what was going on outside."

I could hear myself talking way too much, and way too fast, but I was just so happy to be there.

"Please, sit down," said Mr. B, pointing at a big soft chair next to the warm fireplace.

"Everything is just so—I don't know—pretty, and there's no clutter at all. I can't believe I've never been here, Eleanor; your house is *super cute*."

Eleanor coughed and then asked, "Would you like something to drink?"

"Sure. What've you got?"

"I understand you prefer soda," said Mr. B, "so I bought a bottle of cola for you."

"Not for me, thanks. I guess I forgot to tell you, Eleanor. We've cut out soda at home. I told Mim how the twins drink your water down at the playground, and that you said drinking soda was the same as pouring sugar down your throat, so Mim agreed and stopped buying it, and now we're drinking gallons of chocolate milk. It's delicious and has tons of vitamins."

Eleanor was quiet, like she didn't know what to say. I'm sure she found it hard to believe I didn't want soda, since I used to drink it all the time.

"So very sorry," her father mumbled. "We have neither milk nor chocolate."

He looked like he felt bad about that, so I quickly said, "Oh, anything you have would be great. I love trying new stuff. "

That made him smile again.

"Have you ever tasted coconut water?" he asked. "It's a very popular beverage in our country."

"No, but that sounds delicious!"

Eleanor and I were finally alone together in their family room area while Mr. B went off to get us the drinks. For some reason, Eleanor felt she had to remind me not to say anything about E & R Dream Designs, which I already knew could get her in trouble, because she wasn't allowed to have a job, even though it wasn't technically a job, but I promised her she didn't have to worry a bit about me. I was on my best behavior.

She still looked kind of nervous.

I had lots of questions to ask Mr. B, since Eleanor was always so secretive about her life, like she thought I wouldn't know that her family does a lot of stuff differently from most people because her parents aren't from here. But of course I understood that, and even thought it was awesome, so I truly wanted to know all about it. I've always been very curious about other people and faraway countries.

So after Mr. B returned with the coconut drink, he sat down to talk because dinner was still cooking. And the first thing he said was that *he* wanted to ask *me* a few questions, which made me laugh, since we were obviously thinking alike, and both of us had very curious minds.

"Ruby," he said, "tell me, how go your studies?"

I wasn't quite sure what he meant by that, so I said, "Whaddya mean?"

That's when I noticed that Eleanor was starting to squeeze her hands together, the way she does when things aren't going well. I couldn't figure out what was bothering her so much, since everything seemed great to me.

"Thaththa just wants to know how school is."

"Oh," I replied with a smile. "It's fine. How's the gas business?"

He crinkled up his forehead and frowned a little, and then he shook his head from side to side, and said, "Okay," like he wasn't sure.

Then he asked, "What is your favorite subject to study?"

This was such a typical grown-up question, which honestly made me want to yawn, but I smiled politely and replied, "Well, definitely not gym. Eleanor and I are always coming up with ways of squirming out of that class, unless Ms. Duncan lets us play Ping-Pong, which is the only sport we like. I guess if lunch and recess don't count, then I would have to say Spanish. It's level one, so it's still pretty easy, and Senorita Johnson never gives us any homework."

Mr. B tilted his head and squinted like he was having a hard time understanding *me* this time, so I talked a little slower.

"So how come you and Mrs. B moved to this country? Didn't you like that island where you lived?"

Before her father could answer, Eleanor jumped up and started to cough again, but this time she hacked like she was choking on something, even though we weren't eating anything yet, so I guess her coconut drink went down the wrong tube. I jumped up too and banged on her back.

"Thaththa?" she said in a raspy voice, after she had caught her breath, still coughing a little. "I smell something. Do you think you should check on the curry?"

As soon as her father had disappeared into the kitchen, Eleanor wiggled her finger at me, like she does when she wants me to follow her, and we went into her bedroom. I couldn't believe how much her room reminded me of her, from the pale green walls to the pretty white desk in the corner.

"I thought it would be easier to talk in here for a while and let Thaththa finish making the dinner," she said as we plopped down on her bed.

"Maybe someday we can have a sleepover," I suggested.

Eleanor stared down at her lacy bedspread and picked at loose threads.

"Maybe."

She seemed kind of glum.

"Are you okay?" I asked. "You're awfully quiet, and you keep coughing, and squeezing your hands."

She glanced away. "It's hard to explain."

"Is it about your mother? Is she coming home?"

"Not yet. Nenda Soma isn't any better."

"Are you sad because your amma couldn't see me tonight? Because you don't have to be sad—I'll come back anytime."

Eleanor didn't say anything, so I guessed that was part of what was bothering her. But I didn't know how to cheer her up, so I scanned the room, searching for something special to compliment. That's when I noticed a large, round cardboard box on the floor near the desk. I jumped off the bed and picked it up.

"This is interesting. Where did you get it?"

"Put it down, Ruby!"

I hadn't expected that reaction at all. In fact, I had never seen Eleanor so upset. I slowly placed it back on the floor like it was booby-trapped.

"Sorry," she said. "It's just . . . it's just that"—she was stumbling over her words like she was nervous again—"I keep important things in there. I didn't mean to leave it out."

"Oh, is it where you hide all your yarn and needles and stuff? Or the new rainbow chokers?"

She shook her head. "No, I keep all my knitting supplies in the bottom drawers of my bureau."

Something fishy was going on. My birthday wasn't until the summer, so it couldn't be that. What would she be hiding from me, her best friend?

"By important, do you mean top-secret?"

"It's nothing interesting—really."

Eleanor slid off her bed, pushed the box into the closet, and closed the door.

"Ruby," she said, changing the subject, "the reason I don't have people over to my house is—well, it's complicated."

"Complicated? What's so complicated about your house?" I asked. "I adore your house. And your bedroom is a lot bigger than mine."

"What I'm talking about is . . . it's . . . well, it's more about protocol and traditional customs and appropriate topics of conversation with adults. The ways in which my family interacts are very different from yours. And from everyone else's in Paris."

"What do you mean? Like Christmas and holidays? I know you're Buddish and don't do Christmas. I don't care."

"No, not that exactly. And it's *Buddhist*. Not Buddish."

I had never seen Eleanor act like this. She could normally explain anything; even when she used all sorts of big words to do it, I eventually got what she was trying to say.

"Are you worried about the Monster Chunk cookies? Because I know you only eat vegetables and fish, but there isn't any meat in them. I promise."

"Meat in cookies?"

All at once, Eleanor's eyes widened and she burst out laughing. Eleanor had the best laugh in the whole world when you got her going, and once she started, she had a hard time stopping.

"Who would put meat in cookies?!" she squealed, gasping between each word as she collapsed onto the floor, laughing and clutching her stomach.

"Pardon me, girls?"

Her father had entered the room and stared at Eleanor like she had lost her marbles.

"Is everything all right in here?"

"Don't worry about us, Mr. B! Sometimes all this silliness builds up in Eleanor until she completely cracks up, and then you just have to wait until she gets it out of her system."

Well, you would have thought I'd just said Eleanor won Best Daughter of the Year or something, because her father grinned so hard, I thought he was going to burst too. He swung his arm around me like I was his long-lost cousin.

"Ruby LaRue, you enlighten our world!" he said. "I am so glad you came to dinner. You must come and visit us often."

16

I held hands with Henry and Charlie, one on each side, as we trudged down the unshoveled sidewalk toward Dream Central. I had so much to do today, but we were running late because Mrs. Petite had insisted on throwing our jackets in her dryer to warm them before we headed out into the freezing cold afternoon.

As usual, Eleanor was already sitting at our regular picnic table, but for once she wasn't drawing. Instead she squinted at a tiny piece of paper.

"BOO!"

Eleanor shrieked, then stuffed the note into her pocket without folding it up. And she's the kind of person who neatly folds everything first.

"You startled me," she said.

The boys took off at full speed toward the tall slide.

"What's with you and those notes lately?"

She grinned, but didn't answer, then she studied me up and down.

"What are you looking at?" I asked. "Do I have an icky smudge or a stain?"

"Nope," she replied, "the opposite. You look great."

"I do?" I stared down at my old red boots, trying to figure out what she saw that I didn't.

"I was wondering, Ruby—do you want to go over to The Avalanche and get a mocha ripple milkshake?"

"You can't be serious, Eleanor. Do you have any idea how much I have to get done this afternoon?"

I spread my fingers and began counting off my list of plans.

"After the boys wear themselves out on the playground, I need to drag them all over town, starting with Jenny's Jewelry—BTW, they asked about more crocheted flower earring—then I have to take another order for headbands at the Ski and Snowboard Palace; meet Mrs. Wilder over at the Treasure Chest; and finally, check on the macramé bookmarks at Wonderland's Used Books, all before it's pitch dark and Mim arrives home with dinner."

But instead of commenting on any of that, she said, "I brought an extra banana, if you want one?"

"Sure," I replied, and peeled it without taking off my gloves.

"You know," said Eleanor as she fished around in her backpack, "I wish we knew what happened to Madame Magnifique. I feel like I should knit a gift for her, since her readings were free, and so far everything she predicted is coming true."

"*Ohmygosh*, I've been thinking about that too," I replied, as I watched Eleanor pull out her box of colored pencils and sketchpad, and set them on the table. "How could she appear one day, then vanish into thin air forever? Maybe she really *is* some kind of fairy godmother, you know? Like, she only appears when you *really, really* need her?"

"Normally I would dismiss that line of reasoning," Eleanor said as she began to draw, "but I have to admit, magic could be involved. Otherwise, how could we have accomplished everything we've done so far?"

"I know! It's like she bonked us on our heads with her wand and made our dreams come true."

I took another bite and swallowed.

"Oh, I almost forgot, Ruby—look what I have."

Eleanor dug into her jacket pocket and revealed our latest brainstorm: a pink and purple phone cover that she was modeling on her emergency cell phone.

"Wow, it's wicked cute! We'll sell a million."

"I hope not," she laughed. "Otherwise we'll have to expand and hire staff."

I liked the sound of that: our very own company headquarters.

"By the way, I think I've saved up almost enough money to start ski lessons," I told her. "I need to get really good so I can meet the Outers just like JB did. The Snow Ball's only forty-one days away."

Eleanor didn't say anything, which was always her response when I talked about JB or the Snow Ball. I couldn't understand why she never seemed as excited for my dream as I was for hers, buying that expensive sewing machine. I was beginning to wonder if she was jealous of the idea of me hanging out with the Outers.

"I called Sugar Mountain yesterday to ask how much it would cost."

Still no response as she continued to sketch.

I finished up the banana, then tossed the peel in the trash can.

"Anyway, the lady on the phone said they have this special package, called the Snow Bunny, where you get ski equipment, a private lesson, then a lift pass for the rest of the day, plus a hot chocolate in the lodge, which I can drink by the stone fireplace, just like my real mom did with my pop when they were in high school."

Finally Eleanor looked up.

"How much is the Snow Bunny?"

"For kids under twelve, it's $129, which would still leave me with about fifty bucks left over."

"Wait, Ruby, that doesn't make sense."

"Come on, Eleanor," I said. "Can't you at least be a little happy for me? I mean, it's not like we're going to stop being best friends once I get to know the Outers."

"What are you talking about? I mean, your calculations don't make sense."

She bent over and pulled a notebook from her backpack and flipped through the pages.

"You said $129? And you would only have fifty left? We've made more money than that. What happened to the rest of your profits?"

"Umm . . . I guess most of it went to bribing the twins with junk, like parts for their Clink 'n' Link collections, which I have to buy every time I drag them along to visit our customers, so they'll be quiet and behave."

"But you couldn't have spent that much on Clink 'n' Links. Maybe I made a mistake in my accounting system?"

It was my job to collect our earnings from our customers whenever I dropped off new pieces, and Mim agreed to cash our checks and give us the money. But Eleanor was the one who counted it, recorded it, and then divided it between us down to the last penny.

She flipped to the back of her notebook and pointed at the top of the page.

"So far we've made a total of $540.96 after being in business about ten weeks. We spent $37.42 on various supplies, which leaves us with $251.77 each. I still have to save $268.23, excluding shipping, before I can purchase the Pluckarama online for $520. But Ruby, you should have been able to start your lessons weeks ago."

"Well . . ."

"Well, what?"

"There's also this dress."

"What dress?"

"A *gorgeous* dress, Eleanor! One that I saw in a catalog, which would be *so* perfect for the Snow Ball! It's pure white, which is the color everyone has to wear to look wintry, and it has these puffy princess sleeves, fake fur *all* along the hem, plus tiny clear buttons down the front, which, according to the catalog, 'twinkle like stars at night under the lights!' And I want it *more than anything*. But it's really expensive, and if I spend my money now on ski lessons, I may not have enough left over for the dress."

Eleanor sighed.

"If I only had my sewing machine . . . I could probably make one exactly like it."

All of a sudden, Charlie and Henry ran over, hollering like they were being chased by a flock of wild turkeys.

"HEY! That kid was here!"

"What?" I jumped up and scanned the playground. "Where is he?"

"He ran away when we talked to him," said Charlie as puffs of cold air circled his red cheeks.

"That same boy you saw last month?" asked Eleanor.

"We see him all the time," said Henry.

"You do?" I crossed my arms. "Why didn't you tell me?"

"Because this time he got *really* close."

"And when we asked his name," Charlie said, "he ran off!"

"All right, calm down," I said. "It's not a national emergency, but it *is* a little creepy. Was he wearing the big green jacket?"

"Yep, and a hat squishing his hair down," added Henry.

"It's definitely that rich kid from the mansion. Were binoculars hanging from his neck?"

The boys looked at each other and shrugged, then ran off to chase a squirrel behind a tree.

"The weird thing is," I said to Eleanor, "I haven't seen him outside in his yard for weeks. I wonder what he's up to, and why he keeps sneaking around like this."

"He may be extremely introverted," said Eleanor as she continued to sketch, "or suffer from a social anxiety disorder, or any number of phobias."

"Are you kidding? How can anyone suffer from anything living in a million-dollar mansion?"

"Money doesn't buy happiness, Ruby," she replied, without looking up. "In fact, money has very little to do with happiness other than covering the basic necessities for a reasonably comfortable existence."

Honestly, I don't know where she gets these ideas.

"What are you talking about, Eleanor? Have you seen those Outers? Beautiful, rich, and happier than anyone on earth!"

A cloud passed over the sun, which was low in the sky.

"Who truly knows what an individual feels, or what makes him or her uniquely happy, other than that individual?"

Eleanor stopped drawing and turned her picture around for me to see: a pretty girl in a beautiful white gown.

"That's it!" I said. "The dress in the catalog. How did you do that?"

She smiled one of her extra-curly grins and closed the pad of paper.

"It's getting late, Ruby. You need to call on customers, and I need to crochet phone covers in case we get some orders."

"Shoot, I forgot about my appointments."

I jumped up and called the boys.

"Charlie, Henry, get back here—we gotta go!"

"Wait," said Eleanor. "Don't forget the new phone-cover sample."

Maybe Eleanor and I didn't always think about the world in the same way, but we sure made a great team.

"I'm telling you, these things are gonna sell like ice melt before a storm. Make as many as you can!"

A couple of weeks later, my stepmom arrived home early from the Slope Side Café. It was a Saturday, and she was in an extra good mood because they had sold out of the day's cookie supply by noon, and decided to give her the rest of the day off. Mim's secret recipe was getting more famous every day. Meanwhile, Pop was still on the road and, as far as I could tell, he had no plans to come home soon. I began to worry a little. Why did he need to work so much? It just didn't make sense. Every time I tried to bring it up, Mim changed the subject.

Lately, I had been fussing around the house, cleaning and de-cluttering even more because: 1) It made Mim really happy to have the extra help, which I never knew before because she had never asked; 2) it was a lot easier to keep track of all the stuff I used to misplace; and 3) I don't know why, but I really liked rechecking the clean area over and over again.

So there was Mim, glowing as brightly as the sunlight beaming through the front door.

"Everything looks so nice, Rosebud!" she said. "Why don't you call Eleanor and go have fun for the rest of the day? There's a bluebird sky and the sun feels warm. I bet even the mountains of sugary snow are melting a little."

And that's when I knew I had to take my big chance and ski.

Even though there were just four weeks left until the Snow Ball, I still needed $16 more to purchase the Snow Bunny lesson and, at the same time, have enough money for the beautiful white gown in the catalog, which said to allow three whole weeks for delivery.

I ran through a checklist in my head: It was the weekend, so there was no school. Mim was home early, which meant I didn't have to watch the twins. It was a crystal-clear day. Yep, I was as ready as I was ever going to be. I decided I had to take the risk and splurge on the lesson—and hope that I'd make $16 within the next few days in order to purchase the dress in time.

"That's a good idea, Mim. I'll go by Eleanor's house and surprise her. And maybe Mr. B will invite me over for one of his delicious curry dinners tonight."

I felt kinda bad about fibbing, but I didn't want Mim to know about the ski lesson—not yet. I wasn't sure she would understand.

"Oh, if you're going to stay for dinner, you have to bring something," she said as she searched through the cabinets for gift ideas. "You can't arrive empty-handed. Now let me see what we've got . . ."

She paused and stared at the organized candy shelf.

"Well, doesn't this look delightfully neat. But how come nothing's been eaten? What are you kids having for snacks these days?"

I don't know why, but suddenly I felt a little guilty, like I might get in trouble, even though Mim hardly ever got mad about anything.

"Eleanor usually brings extra food for us to share down at the playground."

"What extra food? We have plenty of stuff here. You shouldn't be eating Eleanor's snacks."

"But she has special food that we don't have."

"Like what?"

"B'nanas!" yelled Charlie from the couch.

My stepmother looked confused.

"What's so special about bananas?"

"It's not just bananas," I said. "Like, sometimes Eleanor has dried mango, which is sweet and chewy, and also nuts, mostly cashews. I don't know what else, but interesting, healthy stuff like that."

Mim's face changed. It was like she had been told something she didn't want to hear.

"That's awfully thoughtful of Eleanor," she said quietly.

My stepmom and I could talk about practically anything. She would offer her warm smile and have a big hug ready, no matter how bad I felt, and she'd be ready with advice if I needed it. But somewhere deep inside of me, I knew I wasn't supposed to talk about this. Food.

"I feel better after eating Eleanor's snacks. Plus I'm hardly wheezing these days."

"Really?"

I nodded. Mim sank down into a kitchen chair.

"Well," she replied, "we already cut out soda. And I can certainly buy nuts."

"And b'nanas," Charlie yelled again.

Mim smiled.

"You're right. We need to plan our food better," she said. "You're growing up so fast, Rosebud, and lately your dad and I are barely around to see it!" She reached for my hand and said, "I'm proud of you, Ruby LaRue."

I wanted to tell Mim I was proud of her too, and that I knew it was exhausting to work so many hours and do practically everything by herself, but it feels funny to say that kind of thing to a grown-up. And I realized I didn't want to know why Pop had been away so long. I just wanted him to come home.

"Now run along and have fun at Eleanor's house, and tell her hello for me, and hello to her father too. Promise you'll call if you decide to stay for supper."

"I promise!"

"And pick up some of that dried fruit as a little gift on your way, okay?"

She pulled a few dollars out of her pocket and stuffed them in my hand.

"Sure, Mim," I said, and hugged her as hard as I could.

It was funny when I thought about it: I'd only been to Sugar Mountain Ski Resort two times in my life, both times when Pop had a weekend off and took me and the twins to visit Mim at the café. Like always, she was crazy busy and barely had time to sneak in a hello since the line was out the door.

Now it felt weird arriving there all by myself. I was painfully aware that my jacket and snow pants didn't match and that my pretty gloves knitted by Eleanor weren't real ski gloves, and I had never even thought about goggles. Maybe I could rent those too.

Everything was so confusing and noisy upstairs in the main part of the lodge. The floors were sopping wet and music pounded too loudly and a voice booming over a speaker was announcing the winners of a race. Normally I loved crowds and never missed a fair or festival in town, but this wasn't the same. It was hard to believe I was still in Paris; it felt like another world.

I finally got up the nerve to ask an Outer walking by (a young mom with a baby, who looked friendly enough) where I needed to go to rent skis. But she didn't answer me. Instead she pointed up at a sign with the word RENTALS and an arrow pointing down toward the basement area.

"I'd like the Snow Bunny ski special," I said to the guy behind the cash register who was standing below another sign that said ENTER HERE.

He leaned toward me and squinted.

"The *what*, dude?"

"Umm . . . I called on the phone a couple weeks ago? And someone told me I could rent everything? And get a first lesson and a ticket and a cup of hot chocolate for $129, because I'm under twelve?"

"Did you book it?"

"Huh?"

"You know, make a reservation for the lesson?"

"No. No one told me to."

He shoved his hair out of his eyes and opened a notebook.

"Lucky for you it's a slow day."

Then he punched a bunch of numbers into the cash register and said, "That's $141.50 total."

"*That much?* But I thought—"

"Tax and service fee," he said.

That meant I would be more than $28 short to buy the dress! But I had to trust that everything would work out. After all, Madame Magnifique's magic had gotten me this far.

My wallet was stuffed with cash, which I counted out carefully down to the two quarters. Mim had offered to open a savings account with me and put my profits in there, but she didn't know that I had plans to use up most of it right away.

The guy took my money and handed over a packet of papers.

"I forgot," he said. "A parent or guardian over the age of twenty-one has to sign this first."

I stared at the pages of tiny words stapled together.

"Sign what?"

He flipped to the last page.

"Permission form. We need a 'John Hancock' from an adult right there, dude, last line. Name and date."

"But no one told me that on the phone either!"

"It's no big deal. Just find your mom upstairs, have her sign it, and come back and get your receipt."

Aaarrggh! I thought to myself. What else could go wrong? I didn't know what to do. But for some reason, today felt like the day I *had to* learn how to ski.

Before I knew it, I found myself rushing back up the stairs and forging my stepmother's name along with the date on the last page, as if someone else were holding the pen. Another little fib.

"Now, here's your tag for your jacket, and don't lose that receipt," said the guy at the register, after I returned the permission packet with the fake signature. "Go to the Red Zone and get fitted for boots and a helmet. Go to the Green Zone to get poles and skis. Then go to the Blue Zone to wait and be assigned an instructor. *Next!*"

Someone pushed against me, so I moved forward down the line. I peered ahead and saw a red square hanging from a chain: The Red Zone.

I followed a man ahead of me whose son kept whining, like he didn't want anything to do with skiing.

"You'll be fine," said the dad. "You can use the bathroom later."

"Size?" said a man behind the counter.

Another guy grabbed the receipt out of my hand before I even noticed him.

"What?" I asked.

"Boot size?"

I glanced down at my feet.

"I don't know."

He leaned over the wooden counter to take a look.

"About a size six shoe?"

"Well, it depends on what I'm wearing. If it's sneakers, I wear a six and a half, but if it's flats—"

He shoved a pair of stiff, plastic, lime-colored boots in my face. I dropped them on the floor, they were so heavy. The piece of paper was stuck in a buckle.

"Don't lose your receipt," he said. "*Next!*"

The man with the cranky boy stood under a green box so I rushed to catch up to them: The Green Zone.

"What level?" said a man with long, tangled, blond hair and a pierced eyebrow. I always wanted to ask people with face piercings if it still hurt after they've had it a while, because it looks so uncomfortable.

"Huh?" I said.

"What level for you?"

"Isn't this the basement?" I asked.

That made him laugh and lean forward on his elbows.

"Have you ever skied before?"

I felt a little embarrassed, but knew I had to be honest about this.

"No, but my father used to ski here all the time."

"Cool," he said.

I liked him. He was the first friendly person I had met so far.

"Listen: I'm gonna give you these skis because they're excellent for your first time out, okay?"

"Okay!" I said, finally relaxing a little and getting excited.

"And here are your poles and your receipt. Now don't lose that receipt."

"I won't!"

I wished I knew his name, because he had been the only nice helper and he was pretty cute and I wanted to ask him a few other questions and maybe see if he'd give me the private lesson, or at least recommend the best teacher.

But then he hollered *Next!* like the other guys had, and that's when I realized I had no idea how to carry all this junk over to the Blue Zone and find my instructor. In fact, I didn't even *see* the Blue Zone, just a door leading outside. And the man and his whiny kid had disappeared too.

Right then, a tall woman with long red hair—wearing bright orange overalls, the same color as one of those traffic cones—waved her hand and hollered, "Who reserved the Snow Bunny Special?"

I glanced behind me and when I didn't hear anyone else speak up, I figured she had to be talking about me.

"I did," I said timidly, but she didn't seem to hear me, so I shouted, "*I did!*"

She whipped her head and long red hair in my direction, then looked me up and down without smiling.

"Follow me," she ordered, and vanished out the side door before I had even picked up one pole.

I don't know how I did it, but I dragged all that equipment outside into the super-sunny-snowy-blue-sky ski world. It was like walking onto a movie set, but a sci-fi movie, set on the moon or something, the way the snow glowed too brightly with everyone shuffling around in moon suits and moon boots.

Hundreds of alien Outers were flying down the steep white hill in front of me, scraping the snow sideways to stop short at the bottom, then sliding by on the flat ground, lining up at the lifts, laughing and gliding perfectly. I was in their world now!

The tall traffic-cone-orange woman towered over me, wearing pointy silver sunglasses and black gloves, which made her look like a moon superhero.

"I'm Page," she said and smirked.

"Like, in a book?" I asked, trying to be super friendly.

"I guess. Who are you?"

"Ruby," I said, dropping all my heavy gear at once in a heap on the ground, "like the color of a rose."

"Where's your helmet, Ruby?" she asked, still not cracking a smile.

"Nobody gave me one."

"I'll be right back," she barked. "In the meantime, get those boots on."

Lying sideways in the snow, the lime-colored ski boots looked more like one of those puzzles that have knots and ropes and hooks and buckles than something you would wear. I noticed a wooden bench next to the door, so I shoved everything toward it and sat down.

Page reappeared with a scratched-up helmet, set it in my lap, knelt in front of me, ripped off my snow boots, and shoved the heavy ski boots onto my feet.

"OW!" I said. It came out louder than I meant it to.

"You'll get used to it," Page mumbled, as she snapped all the buckles into place.

I didn't know how I would walk in those tight things, let alone ski.

"Where's your receipt?" she asked as she stood up. "I have to sign off on it so you can get your lift ticket after your lesson and ski the rest of the day."

"And the cup of hot chocolate by the stone fireplace too," I said as I handed over the mashed piece of paper. But she didn't seem to hear that part.

"We'll go over the basics at the bottom here on flat ground, then we'll take the rope tow up the bunny hill and practice your snowplow. Got it?"

I scanned the amazing moon world of fabulousness, home of my deepest dreams, then took a deep breath and yelled, "Got it, Page!"

"What is it?" cried Eleanor, throwing open her front door.

"OH, ELEANOR!" I blubbered. "EVERYTHING IS RUINED!!"

I collapsed facedown in her hallway—my red snow boots sticking out the door—and howled louder than a coyote.

"Ruby, what are you talking about? What's happened?! The back of your jacket is torn!"

But beyond that, I couldn't hear what Eleanor was saying as I sobbed and sobbed and sobbed.

She bent down in front of me and pulled at my arms.

"Roll over and talk to me!" she insisted. "I need to close the door, Ruby."

I inched my body forward, but couldn't stop my sobbing, which was turning into gasping, choking noises. My face was so hot and damp, it stung.

"Ahh! *Were you skiing at Sugar Mountain?*" Eleanor demanded as she tugged on the ski pass attached to one of my jacket pockets.

I wailed louder.

In another room, the phone rang.

"Oh, *aiyo!*" said Eleanor. "I'll be right back—don't go *anywhere.*"

Eventually, between crying spasms, my tears slowed and I suddenly felt extremely tired. If I hadn't been lying in the middle of someone else's hallway, I think I would have fallen into a deep sleep right then and there.

Instead, I forced myself to stand, take off my boots, and find Eleanor, whose quiet voice was coming from the kitchen.

Every part of my body ached.

I found her leaning against the sink, talking softly on the phone in Sinhala. She turned around slowly to look at me and gasped out loud, as if I'd frightened her, then said a few more quick foreign words into the phone and hung up.

"Who was that?" I managed to ask between sniffles.

"Amma," Eleanor replied quietly. "Nenda Soma is much better now. So my mother is flying home tomorrow night."

More bad news! I mean, even though it should be a good thing that Nenda Soma was better and that Eleanor's mom was returning after being away for so long, I knew it really meant that all the fun we had been having would come to a screeching halt.

I just couldn't take it on top of my already *hideous* day, and I burst into tears all over again.

Eleanor took my hand, led me into their family room, and pushed me down into their soft comfortable chair where I curled up into a tight ball. She set a box of tissues on the coffee table.

"Where's your thaththa?" I managed to ask between sobs, grabbing a wad of tissues to wipe my whole face.

"He's still at the gas station."

She touched a spot on my cheek and it hurt.

"*Ow!*"

"Oh, Ruby," Eleanor whispered, and took a deep breath. "Tell me what happened. Please?"

I forced myself to look up and absorb the Bandaranaikes' sweet house with all their beautiful decorations from their island country, and I tried to think about how nice it would be to visit that island country with its delicious food and colorful birds and tropical jungles. And I did this until my heartbeat finally calmed down and I managed to stop crying.

"I knew I needed to"—*hic*—"take my lesson soon"—*hic*—"and since it was a sunny day and Mim got"—*hic*—"home early to watch the boys"—*hic*—"I rushed over to Sugar Mountain before I could change my mind"—*hic*—"even though I didn't have enough"—*hic*—"money for the gown in the catalog"—*hic*—"yet."

"Wait," said Eleanor. "I'll make some tea. Take off your jacket, Ruby, and I'll be right back."

When Eleanor stood up, something fell from the back pocket of her pants. Another piece of paper folded into a tiny square. I gazed blankly at it as if my brain had completely shut down.

Soon after, the whistle on the kettle blew and Eleanor returned with a tray of tea stuff, which she set on the coffee table. She saw me staring at the tiny paper on the floor and quickly picked it up.

I took another tissue and blew my nose hard.

"Why are you dropping so many notes lately, Eleanor?"

At first she wouldn't look at me, like she felt ashamed of something.

"They're nothing, really," she replied. "Tell me your story first, and then I'll explain."

"You're like a mother, you know," I said, and even smiled a little, "making tea and taking care of me."

Eleanor smiled back and patted my knee, then sat on the floor near my feet.

"So did you take a lesson?" she asked.

"Sort of. I rented the ski gear, which I'm telling you, there's a lot of, and it's hard to walk in those moon boots, lugging everything, and the helmet feels like a boulder on your head. Anyway, I followed Page, the super *unfriendly* instructor, to the beginner area, where they have this picture of a bunny on a sign, which stands for the bunny hill, which is the easiest hill where they teach people, but believe me, it's not that easy. Skiing is a *lot* harder than it looks!"

Eleanor leaned back against the wall and sipped her tea. I could tell she was listening carefully because that's the kind of friend Eleanor is.

"So, rude Page shoved my boots into my skis and showed me how to hold the poles and then talked about 'french fries' and 'pizza,' which is the way you learn to ski down the hill. She said she would call out 'french fries' when she wanted my skis straight ahead, like two french fries, and when she yelled 'pizza,' that meant I had to snowplow so the tips of my skis were touching together, to look like a wedge of pizza.

"Then we practiced on the flat ground until I got it, and finally we went up the rope tow, which also looks a lot easier than it really is. You can't grab it like I did the first time, because it will yank you down to the ground until you fall on your face and the rope stops and everyone is stuck waiting for you to get up."

"Oh no," said Eleanor. "Is that how you cut your cheek?"

"What's wrong with my cheek?"

Eleanor scrunched up her nose.

"Umm, nothing; just a little scrape. Go on with your story."

"Anyway, once I got the hang of the rope tow and we made it to the top, I was shocked to see how long and steep the bunny slope really is, because standing at the bottom and looking up the hill, it hardly looked like a bump. Page told me to follow her over to the far side by marching on my skis and pounding the poles. Most of the younger kids were attached to adults skiing down behind them with these harnesses, like they were little ponies, but Page said I shouldn't have to wear one at my age, as long as I listened to her instructions."

I had to stop and take a deep breath, because this is where it got hard to talk about.

"That's when I should have asked Page more questions, but something about her made me so nervous, Eleanor. It wasn't the fact that she didn't even know *how* to smile or say something nice, but it was the way she was rushing, like she didn't have time for me—like she had crammed unimportant me between other really important things, even though I had paid all that money we worked so hard for! So instead of getting everything straight and asking her to repeat stuff, I waited for her to give me orders, like I was in the army."

"Sounds like my cello teacher."

"Really?"

I had forgotten all about my tea and bent over to take a sip.

"She's dreadful," said Eleanor. "But tell me, what happened next?"

At that point I had a very difficult time keeping my voice steady. I didn't want to start crying again, so I took a couple more sips of tea and swallowed hard.

"Well, I waited sideways at the top of the hill while Page explained that she would give me a *little* push on my back to get me going, and then follow right down next to me, saying either 'french fries' or 'pizza,' and that I was supposed to copy her and make the right shapes when she said it all, the same way we had done it at the bottom of the hill."

I paused to take a big gulp of tea, followed by a deeper breath. But my voice kept getting higher and my words shakier.

"So I did that, only I pushed down on the poles the same time she gave me a HUGE shove, *not* a little push like she said, and before I knew it I was flying downhill on french-fry skis! I could hear Page's voice yelling 'PIZZA! PIZZA!,' but I couldn't push my toes together to make a pizza wedge, so that meant I couldn't stop my skis, and the whole time my arms were making circles and my poles were flinging out to my sides and I thought I would fall backwards, but somehow I kept going and going straight, all the way to the bottom—*and right before I got there* I saw this big group of Outer girls strolling by in their fancy jackets, holding their fancy skis and snowboards, *and I screamed* so they could jump out of the way, but they just stared up at me and screamed back and I plowed right into them and we all landed in a giant HEAP!!"

Eleanor quietly repeated, "A *heap?*"

"BUT THAT'S NOT THE WORST PART!" I said, as I exploded into sobs again.

Now Eleanor's whole face puckered up like she had swallowed a lemon.

"It isn't?"

"OH, ELEANOR!! Those Outer girls were so mean. They started calling me *swear* words I can't even *say*, and even after they stood up, they kept yelling down at me, because I couldn't stand up with my skis tangled between my legs. One of them called me *lardo*, even though all my clothes are wicked loose now, and another Outer told me to get my *townie* butt off her boot. But worst of all, when I focused and stared up at them, I realized they weren't all girls. One of them was *JB Knox!* And he was bent over, moaning in pain, practically crying!"

Eleanor gasped. "Oh, Ruby."

"And stupid, rude Page didn't even care that *I* was flat on the ground, in pain. She kept apologizing to the horrible *Outers* and said nothing to me and put her arm around JB, asking him if he was okay, and left me there *without asking if I was okay*, and then she took JB back to the lodge or somewhere and the Outer girls said more wicked mean stuff, like I ruined his basketball career FOREVER!! *Plus . . .*"

I couldn't say it. Eleanor reached up and patted my back.

"Plus what, Ruby?"

"*Plus . . .* I never got to drink hot chocolate by the stone fireplace like my mom and pop used to do when they were in high school."

And with that, I erupted into full blubbering. A volcano of humiliating lava-spewing tears sprayed all over the family room.

I knew this had to have been the most horrendous story Eleanor had ever heard, because it was the worst thing that could possibly happen to anyone.

"Oh, Ruby," she said, "I was afraid—*really afraid*—that something like this might happen. Maybe some dreams just aren't meant to come true."

And then she spread a blanket across my lap and whispered, "I'll boil some more water."

Eleanor was right. I had reached too high. And now my dream had become a nightmare.

I had no reason to go to the Snow Ball, or anywhere else, ever again.

I had never imagined in a million years that people could be so cruel over an accident. Most of all, I was shocked to find out that the Outers went to all that trouble to appear like perfect, happy people when the truth was, they were the opposite. They were bullies.

Eleanor had been right about them too. I hadn't allowed myself to believe anything bad about those Outers as they trotted around Paris in their phony, beautiful-people herd.

And JB! I was even more hurt by *his* horribleness, and not only because I had *had* a humongous crush on him, but because he had been so nice to me before, and then ignored me like I'd ruined his entire life on purpose. I mean, wouldn't you think a kid who plays sports all the time gets injured once in a while?

Then, to make matters even worse, I was grounded for two weeks.

Since I was having a major meltdown at Eleanor's house, I forgot all about calling Mim to tell her where I was—although I never did get an invite for dinner, since Mr. B was running late at work. But I did stay over there, crying my eyes out and drinking gobs of tea, until about six o'clock, and then I'd stumbled home in the dark, which I'm technically not allowed to do—walk alone in the dark, I mean—so that was the real reason I got grounded.

Plus, when Mim saw my face with the gash that I didn't even know was that bad, because Eleanor had acted like it was nothing (probably to keep me from feeling worse), she freaked out! I exploded into tears again and told her everything about spending my profits on the skiing lesson only to crash into people on my first time down the hill. Except I didn't tell her the part about having a crush on JB, or the part about wanting to be friends with the Outers (neither of which was even a teensy bit true anymore), and especially not the part about forging her signature—so she couldn't figure out why I went to all that trouble without telling her.

I tried to explain that I just wanted to learn how to ski before the Snow Ball so I could fit in, but she told me Pop could have taught me all about skiing, and it wouldn't have cost me a dime.

Except for the fact that he's never around anymore.

And then, on top of everything, I found out that Eleanor got into tons of trouble too.

I phoned her the next morning to let her know about my punishment, but she told me she could only talk a few minutes, and she sounded wicked upset.

It turned out her thaththa had been late getting home the night before because he'd had some errands to do in town, and he had discovered that Eleanor and I had this major company. We never thought he would ever find out about it, because Mr. B only goes to the grocery store and the hardware store, and not the types of shops where we sell our E & R line.

But on Saturday after work, he went into the Treasure Chest for the first time to buy a wedding gift for one of his gas station mechanics, and he recognized some of the little knitted items he had seen Eleanor working on in the evenings. He asked the owner, Mrs. Wilder, where she got them, and she enthusiastically told him all about these two smart and talented girls who ran their own business and how their creations were selling like "hotcakes," and that they would be self-made millionaires any day now. That was super nice of Mrs. Wilder to say, but a huge exaggeration, which, as Eleanor said, only fueled Mr. B's angry flame.

Mr. B bought one of the new cell-phone covers, then showed it to Eleanor when he arrived home, insisting she explain why she had gone behind his back and gotten a job. Which, of course, took Eleanor completely by surprise; she hadn't prepared anything to say in case this happened.

She ended up confessing, though she tried to explain to her father that she didn't think of it as a job, but as a fun way of making money to save up for the Deluxe Electronic Pluckarama 1080 Sew-Good & Embroidery Machine, so she could someday create her own fashion line.

"But how do you run a business?" her thaththa asked. "Do your customers write checks? Who cashes them?"

"Oh no," I said to Eleanor on the phone. "Mim."

"I had to tell him, Ruby. I couldn't lie anymore."

So *I* had to confess to Mim that Eleanor's father hadn't exactly been aware of E & R Dream Designs, which made her even angrier.

And on top of everything, Eleanor's mother was flying home that night, so Eleanor was extra worried about getting in a hundred times more trouble for everything.

IT WAS ALL SO DEPRESSING.

Somehow I managed to drag myself to school on Monday morning, since I knew I couldn't hide forever. It was hard enough to go, feeling physically and emotionally sore from the bunny slope accident, but then I nearly fainted when I spotted JB with his right arm in a sling. He was getting more attention in the hallways than he had after making the half-court shot last winter that won the county basketball tournament.

And just to make sure the whole world knew about my klutziness, I found out some of those Outer girls had posted pictures of me—tangled up in my skis—all over the Internet. For once I was grateful I didn't have my own phone or laptop.

As you can imagine, the only thing I had been looking forward to on this horrible Monday was seeing Eleanor *in person* to complain about all our fiascos together at school during lunch, since we always seemed to figure out the answer to everything together. But I was shocked to find out from Anton in the cafeteria line that she was absent!

I couldn't remember the last time Eleanor had missed school, but I really hoped her absence had nothing to do with her amma going bonkers from Eleanor's winter of freedom and getting a job—I mean, what if she punished Eleanor and then decided to schedule even more lessons and activities?

I had never felt so completely alone.

After hearing the horrible news from Anton and paying the cafeteria lady, I stared down at my tray of food and thought about throwing it in the trash and escaping out the door. I had no idea where I would go . . . just anywhere but here.

"So, did you cut your face skiing?" Anton asked.

I glanced up at him and scowled.

That was it. I couldn't take it anymore, especially not from Anton Orlov.

"You know, it looks kinda cool," he said, as he followed me over to the garbage cans. "Like you're, you know, *tough*. Like no one better mess with you."

I paused before the recycling bins and turned toward him.

He was grinning, but not in a mean way, and that's when I remembered how he'd helped Lewis.

"Are you making fun of me," I mumbled, "or do you mean that?"

He took a deep breath and shook his head.

"Come on, Ruby. Come on over and sit with us."

The empty seat where Eleanor always sat next to me at lunch made me feel worse than anything that had happened in the last couple of days, as if she had disappeared and was never coming back. But I was grateful to Anton for somewhere to sit when it felt like the rest of the world was against me. I guess I had been wrong about him—and a lot of other things—all along.

Somehow I survived the rest of that miserable Monday at school without running away, which probably would have landed me with detentions for the rest of my life from Mr. Tankhorn.

Later, as I slogged through the cold, sad, snowy streets toward Mrs. Petite's house to pick up the twins—feeling *sooooo* sorry for myself—I turned onto Bon Hiver Lane and suddenly noticed that the rich kid was in front of his mansion, looking through his binoculars.

I hadn't seen him out in his yard for more than a month, but I felt so depressed that I didn't even have the energy to stop and call him over and ask questions, which he wouldn't have answered anyway. So I continued on past the black metal gates.

But then he called over to me: "Ruby LaRue!"

I couldn't help turning around, even though I wasn't in the mood to talk to anyone.

"Hey," I moaned, and gave a tiny wave.

He ran toward me in his green jacket, which instantly reminded me of his spying down at Dream Central.

"Where've *you* been?" I snapped, feeling angry all over again.

He stopped short and his binoculars bounced against his jacket. "What?"

"I haven't seen you in a while. Where've you been hiding?"

"Florida," he said, like he wasn't sure, staring down at his feet.

"*Florida?* For how long?"

"Since our arrival at two thirty-six p.m. on January eighth. We stayed at our house in Naples."

I glanced over at the mansion behind him and asked, "How many houses do you own?"

"I don't own any, but my parents have several."

I had never known anyone who owned two houses, let alone "several," other than my uncle George, who has a regular house and then a cabin on a brook, so he can get away and go fishing, and also a hook-up camper for his pickup truck, but I'm not sure if that counts.

"Well, if you were in Florida," I demanded to know, "then how come you were spying on us down at the playground?"

He finally looked up at me, squinting into the dull sun.

"I don't understand."

"Don't pretend you don't know what I'm talking about. You know exactly what I'm saying."

He glanced over his right shoulder, like he was looking for an answer.

"This is confusing me," he said.

"What's so confusing? I invited you to hang out with all of us, my little brothers, Eleanor, and me. So why did you have to hide in the bushes and stalk us like a creep?"

He mumbled something.

"*What?* I can't hear you!"

"I don't understand your framework of reference," he explained a little louder. "I was in Florida until yesterday, when we returned at six fifty-three on a nonstop flight to Manchester-Boston Regional Airport, gate twelve, baggage carousel B."

Then he kicked at the ground and made a beeline for the giant front door, as usual, without saying anything else, except I could tell he was extra upset by the way he stomped through the snow.

All of a sudden I felt bad, like I had forced him to lie in detail about being in Florida. Obviously, he had to be the one who'd been spying on us at the playground; he just didn't think he'd ever get caught. Except I was mean about it, snapping at him and not giving him a chance to tell the truth. I was no better than those stupid Outer bully girls.

But none of it mattered anymore, since Dream Central was permanently in the past, along with my dreams of the Snow Ball and that awful JB Knox. Honestly, I didn't care much about anything, especially being friends with some strange, rich kid.

I took my time walking over to the Petites' house, still wondering how my life went from *okay-but-kinda-boring* to *super-exciting-dreams-can-come-true* to *worse-than-ever* so quickly. I guess life can be like that. If Mim hadn't been so upset with me, she would have said the trick was looking on the bright side of every situation, seeing partly sunny when the forecast said partly cloudy.

But right now I couldn't see a bright side. Only dark gray clouds spitting endless snow at my face.

Winter was no longer my favorite season. It had practically ruined my life.

"Ruby," said Mrs. Petite as soon as she opened her front door, "Charlie and Henry seem a tad sluggish, dear. Now, I took their temperatures, which were both normal, but thought I should mention it. Could be the seasonal blues. You know, the lack of sunshine."

"I think we've all got that problem, Mrs. Petite," I said, "but thanks for mentioning it."

The three of us dragged slowly back to our house, since there was no rush to go anywhere or do anything anymore. I felt sad that the boys seemed almost as down as I did. The twins knew Mim was upset with me, which meant they were punished too, since we all had to stay inside.

"I don't get it," Charlie whined as we made our way up the driveway. "Why can't we go to the playground anymore?"

"I told you already: I'm grounded, which means I can't go anywhere, which means you can't go anywhere. Plus there's no reason to go to the playground, since Eleanor is in trouble like me."

"Are you and Eleanor going to jail?" asked Henry.

"No," I said, "even though it feels like we're in prison right now."

Somehow, my life had offered me a thrilling $50,000 Showcase Showdown, like I had been a finalist on *The Price Is Right*, but then the contestant next to me had beaten me with a perfect guess, winning everything, and leaving me with the big nothing I'd started with.

In fact, I was right back to where I had been before we met Madame M: picking up the twins at Mrs. Petite's house, only to haul them home to watch reruns on television, and eat leftover Monster Chunk cookie pieces. Except now I wasn't looking forward to any of it, not even one teensy bit. It felt wrong this time around.

I had seen the other side of an interesting life—a reason to get up every morning and create something out of nothing with my very best friend. I admit, reaching our dreams had seemed impossible most of the time, but still, I had loved every minute of trying.

When we got to the house, I immediately saw the blinking light on the answering machine. I hoped it was Eleanor. Or maybe even Pop saying he was finally on his way home. But it was messages from store customers wanting new E & R Dream Designs to sell.

I had no idea what to do. Was I supposed to go around to every shop and tell them that the company had gone belly-up because all of our dreams had been ruined in one day?

I grabbed the bag of leftover cookie chunks that was still sitting on the counter from Saturday, clicked on the television set, and plopped down on the couch between the boys. But none of us said or ate a thing.

And *The Price Is Right* was completely smushy.

MARCH

The next morning I felt so relieved to see Eleanor in gym class for second period that I practically gave her a big bear hug in the locker room.

But she was acting so weird, like she wasn't herself at all. Slumped on a bench and staring down at the tiled floor, she hadn't even changed into her gym clothes.

"Eleanor, are you okay?" I whispered so no one would notice. I'd had enough negative attention for a lifetime.

"Why were you absent yesterday?" I asked, slipping next to her on the bench. "I was dying to call you after school, but didn't know if you were allowed to talk on the phone."

Eleanor said nothing. She continued to sulk, her arms folded across her chest.

"Oh, Eleanor, I wished you'd been here. It was possibly the worst day of my life, at least as bad as Saturday. That dumb JB Knox got so much pity for his broken arm in a sling. And people who I don't even know said such mean things to me—as mean as those Outer girls. I almost ran away. But then luckily Anton asked me to sit with him and the Math Squad at lunch, even though you weren't around. Actually, Anton was pretty nice to me for once, but otherwise, it feels like I'm the most hated person in the entire school."

I could tell Eleanor was listening, because she tilted her head toward me a little. But at the same time she crossed her legs tighter, like she was trying to twist her whole body up into one big knot.

After the misery I'd been through, I couldn't bear to think that Eleanor also blamed me for everything that had gone wrong with her life.

"Don't tell me you're mad at me, too? Is that why you're acting so strange, Eleanor?"

I bent down close to her so I could see if her lips were moving.

Very slowly, she shook her head back and forth.

"What is it then? Are you feeling sad or mad because your amma came home, and you're back to your crazy schedule?"

Again she signaled no, which surprised me. I thought for sure her mother was driving her crazy.

"Well then, is it about your thaththa discovering E and R Dream Designs, and not getting to buy your sewing machine? I guess your deepest dream turned into a nightmare too."

But it was no, again.

I couldn't think of anything else that could be troubling her enough to make her act like this. After all, weren't all those things horrible enough?

That's when Ms. Duncan blew her whistle.

"Free morning!" she called. "I've got to write up evaluations, so you're free to play at any station, girls."

This was the best news I'd heard in days. Everyone cleared out quickly to grab their favorite activities.

"Did you hear that, Eleanor? We can play Ping-Pong if you hurry up and change. I'll save us a table."

But she didn't move.

"Eleanor?" I said again, whispering very softly, and then I shook her shoulder.

Ms. Duncan appeared in front of us, scowling.

"What's going on over here, ladies?"

She bent down in front of Eleanor, her hands planted on her knees, and stared up into her face like she was examining a wad of gum stuck under a desk.

"Don't you want to play Ping-Pong?" she asked. "I've noticed you two are pretty good at it."

I had no idea Ms. Duncan thought we were good at anything, but Eleanor still didn't reply, and only scrunched up harder.

"I don't think she's feeling too well," I said. "I've never seen her like this."

Ms. Duncan straightened up and scratched out a note on her clipboard. Then she handed it to me.

"Accompany her to the nurse's office, so she can lie down."

Ms. Duncan also must have realized that something was seriously wrong with Eleanor, because her usual answer to everything was to go sit on the bleachers, even if you thought you were going to barf.

Somehow I managed to untangle Eleanor's arms and pull her to a standing position.

We slipped out without anyone noticing us, and she followed me slowly down the empty hallways, her head tipped at a strange angle. Even though I still felt pretty awful myself, I could only think about Eleanor. I couldn't imagine what could be making her feel so rotten.

The nurse wasn't in her office, but since we had the permission slip, I told Eleanor it was okay to lie down on the cot anyway, and I rolled one of those spinny chairs on wheels close to her.

My pop always tells me I have the gift of gab, so I decided to start babbling to take her mind off things. But as soon as I opened my mouth, she peered up at me from the pillow.

Her eyes were watery and swollen, as if holding back a flood of tears.

"Oh, Eleanor. What's the matter?" I asked one more time. "You can tell me anything. I *promise* I won't tell anyone."

She took a long, deep breath and murmured, "A boy."

I was confused.

"A boy?"

And then she added, "The notes."

Those tiny pieces of paper that had been dropping out of her pockets all winter long . . . She never had explained, and now I knew that something bad was going on.

"Oh, Eleanor, has someone been wicked mean to you, too? Are you being harassed? Or did you get into more trouble with your parents?"

She rubbed and rubbed her eyes with her bony fists, then took another long, deep breath.

"I've been receiving secret notes in my locker from a boy who likes me," she said, pronouncing each word carefully, like she might drop one and break it.

"Wait. What?"

"Notes of admiration from an anonymous source."

"Do you mean, like, *love letters?*"

She nodded.

"But that's so cool, Eleanor! Why would that upset you? Oh wait—are they from someone you don't like? Are they from Anton?"

She sat up on the edge of the bed and sighed.

"I had no idea who they were from, because they were signed NA, for 'Nameless Admirer.' But I knew all along Anton couldn't have written them."

"Why not?"

She shrugged. "I don't know; they were so . . ."

"They were so *what*, Eleanor?"

"For once, I can't find the right words," she said. "Sweet? Funny? Kind?"

What was wrong with this girl?

"I don't get it, Eleanor. What's this got to do with you feeling worse than I've ever seen you feel in your entire life? I mean, Eleanor! *Who wouldn't want to get secret love notes from a secret admirer?* Even if they *were* from Anton."

Eleanor sighed.

"In his very last note NA told me he wasn't going to write them anymore, because he wanted to reveal himself. And that if I wanted to know his identity, I had to meet him under the large maple tree at the entrance to Sugar Mountain."

"You mean the old Sugar Tree? That's *so* romantic! Just like something out of a movie."

Eleanor gazed down at the floor.

"Well, what happened?" I asked. "Did you meet him?"

"I did."

"*When?*"

"On Sunday, two days ago. Later, after you called me on the phone, but before Thaththa and I left for the airport."

"You went alone? Are you crazy, Eleanor? Meeting a stranger like that?"

A million things raced through my head. Did this boy end up being some creep? Or even worse, did he hurt her?"

"It's not what you're imagining," she said. "From what he said in his notes, I knew he was a student at our school. He kept telling me I would recognize him as soon as I saw him. He even suggested the Sugar Tree because it was out in the open and lots of people would be driving by. So I would feel safe."

"Still, you should have gone with someone."

She nodded. "I know. I wasn't thinking clearly. And I had to rush in time to leave for the airport."

"So? Who was it?"

Eleanor covered her eyes and continued her story without looking at me.

"As I approached the entrance to the mountain, I could see the back of someone leaning against the old maple tree. He wore a long green jacket and a dark hat."

"Huh? You mean, like the rich kid who's been spying on us at the playground?"

Eleanor nodded.

"But he doesn't go to our school. And you've never even met him."

"No, not him, Ruby, but the same description. This boy, the one who wrote the notes and probably also the one spying on us," Eleanor paused and squeezed her eyes shut, "had his right arm in a sling."

"A sling? But the only person who . . ."

And then it hit me.

JB Knox.

I walked even slower on my way home from school that cold, blustery afternoon.

Soon, I would be crawling home.

Nothing seemed to make sense to me.

Nothing.

The world had turned upside down and inside out. Somehow, I needed to figure out how to make things right again. But I didn't know if I cared enough anymore.

Back in the nurse's office, Eleanor told me about all the "Nameless Admirer" notes she had received from JB over the winter— thirty-five in all! She had stored them in that round box in her bedroom, the one she told me to put down because it contained something special. She confessed she had lost one note, but wasn't surprised as she dropped them all the time. They made her nervous for tons of reasons, but mostly she knew she would get in big trouble if her parents ever found out about them.

That's when I remembered the folded piece of paper under our couch, signed *NA*.

"Something about a yellow or red shirt?"

Eleanor's eyes bugged out of her head.

"How did you know?!"

"I found it on the floor at my house, but thought it was a note Pop had written before a road trip. What did it mean?"

"I was to wear a yellow shirt if my answer was yes, that I liked getting the notes. And a red shirt if I wanted him to stop writing."

"Oh," was all I could say, still in shock by what it all meant.

"Do you still have it—the note?" Eleanor asked.

"Sorry," I mumbled. "I threw it away."

She touched my arm.

"Good. I threw them all away too."

"You did? Why?"

"After the way he treated you, Ruby, in front of all those Outers? I burned the notes in our fireplace as soon as my parents went to bed on Sunday."

I tried to smile, touched by Eleanor's loyalty, but inside I felt miserable about it all . . . especially the part about Eleanor not telling me. She said she'd enjoyed receiving the mysterious notes, as if they were clues in a game. And that she preferred imagining who could be writing such nice things rather than having their secret identity revealed. But she knew if she told me about them I would insist we figure it out . . . which I probably would have. Most of all, she didn't want to hurt my feelings, worried that I'd be jealous. I told her that was silly, that I would have been happy for her. But the truth is, she was right. I couldn't have dreamed up anything more romantic than receiving tiny secret love notes at the bottom of my locker.

Eleanor said she had assumed all along that one of the Math Squad boys, one of the quieter ones she didn't know that well, was her nameless admirer. Never in a million years did she believe it could be anyone popular or older, or both.

But as she had hurried down the long road to Sugar Mountain to meet NA, she knew the person waiting under the old Sugar Tree couldn't be anyone from the math team. For one thing, this boy was taller than anyone in our grade, but more than that, there was something about the way he casually leaned against the tree, facing the other way, that made him seem confident and cool.

Eleanor approached as quietly as she could—but when she stopped, the crunching of her boots also stopped, which made the boy turn around. The first thing she noticed was his arm in a sling . . .

"Surprised to see me?" JB asked her.

Eleanor couldn't speak, so she nodded.

He pointed at his broken arm.

"Had a little mishap on the slopes yesterday, but I wanted to keep our date."

"A little mishap?" she managed to say. "You mean, the accident? With Ruby?"

"Is that her name?" he asked. "I knew she looked familiar. Your friend needs skiing lessons."

At this point in the story, I had to interrupt Eleanor.

"Wait. Are you saying that JB doesn't even know who I am?"

Eleanor looked down at the floor of the nurse's office and shook her head.

"But I don't get it," I said. "Why has he been so friendly to me lately?"

"I told you," she replied, "a person like that uses everyone else as a mirror, seeing only his own reflection. A total narcissist."

I was still confused.

"Then what about the secret notes? You said they were sweet and funny and kind!"

She shrugged and replied, "They were. But now I know they were also manipulative and opportunistic."

"Oh, Eleanor, in English, *please*."

She rubbed her forehead as if trying to find the right words.

"JB says what he needs to say in order to get what he wants. He pretended to be nice to you at the time, only because he wanted to see me."

"But . . . he never even talked to you."

Eleanor tilted her head. "In a way, he did."

That's when everything changed and my whole body, still sore from the crash, ached even more.

Eleanor stood.

"Sorry. I shouldn't have told you, Ruby. Let's go back to gym class."

"No," I said, and took a deep breath. "I want to hear the rest of the story. What happened after that?"

She looked away. "Let's just forget about it, Ruby."

"Tell me, Eleanor," I said. "I need to know everything."

So Eleanor said she suddenly suspected JB was playing some kind of mean prank on her. That there had to be an explanation for why the most popular boy in the entire middle school had a crush on *her*. She had scanned the entrance to Sugar Mountain, looking to see if some of his friends were also in on the joke, hiding nearby.

But then JB had touched her hand and slipped something into her palm, a small folded note just like all the others. He waited while she read it to herself.

Will you please go to the Sugar Mountain Snow Ball with me?

Neither Eleanor nor I said anything for a moment. We were frozen in place. I even felt a little dizzy, like maybe I should lie down on the cot now. But as soon as I noticed Eleanor's eyes filling up again with tears, I wrapped my arm around her shoulders.

I told her that I could easily believe her nameless admirer was someone as incredibly popular and hot as JB. Because she was the nicest, smartest, prettiest, most interesting girl in the whole school. And that I knew a lot of other people thought so too.

She wiped her eyes and gave me a hug, which she had never done before.

"So are you going to go to the Snow Ball with him?" I asked.

"Oh, Ruby, of course not—that was your dream. I would never, *ever* take that away from you."

I smiled. "Believe me, it's not my dream anymore."

Even though I was relieved that everything was okay between Eleanor and me, I still felt dreadful inside as I plodded down the icy sidewalk through the freezing wind. Nothing in my life had been as it seemed. Or had I just not been paying close enough attention to everything and everyone around me? Could I only see my rosy version of how I wanted things to be, which wasn't the way things really were?

Maybe it was a bad thing to be glass-half-full Ruby.

The cold wind blew so hard I had to stop and turn away from it to catch my breath. My entire body felt numb. I bent over to try and adjust my socks that had slipped low in my snow boots, but I couldn't reach them with my thick gloves. I realized that was exactly how I felt. Like a cold, lonely sock crushed at the bottom of a boot.

But then I remembered this was my favorite pair of socks, my extra-thick striped socks I had lost months ago, the same day Eleanor and I had met Madame Magnifique. Mim had discovered them hidden behind the dryer on Sunday, the morning after my doomed ski lesson. In a weird way, these socks felt like long-lost friends. And knowing that I still had them, that they hadn't been lost forever, made me feel a teensy bit better about my life.

"For your information, I WAS IN FLORIDA!"

The rich kid was standing behind the black iron fence, gripping two posts with his hands, like a trapped gorilla behind bars at a zoo. His binoculars were swinging back and forth from his neck against his green jacket. His messy hair stuck out of his hat. Until he'd yelled at me, I hadn't noticed I was in front of his mansion at the corner of Maine Street and Bon Hiver Lane.

"Yeah, I know that now."

He dropped his hands down by his sides.

"And I wasn't spying on you."

I nodded. "Yep, you weren't."

I definitely didn't have the strength to deal with one more upset person, but deep down I knew I had to apologize to this kid. I had been as mean to him as everyone else had been to me.

"It turned out to be a seventh grader, JB Knox, who happens to have a jacket like yours. Believe me, JB is about the last person I could ever imagine spying, but he wasn't spying on me. He was watching my friend, Eleanor, because he has this huge crush on her. Anyway, I'm sorry about all that . . . umm . . . whatever your name is."

I could tell he hadn't expected me to apologize, because he stared at me, still tensed up, like he had a long list of stuff to complain about.

Then he mumbled, "Lance."

I pulled my hat above my ears to hear him better.

"What did you say?"

"My first name," he spoke a little louder, "is Lance."

"Oh."

The frosty wind suddenly stopped blowing and a slice of purply-blue sky peeked through the clouds.

"Did you have fun in Florida, Lance?"

He kicked lightly at the fence post.

"I hate Florida."

"You do? But how can anyone hate warm, sunny Florida with all those beautiful beaches? I'm so sick of being buried alive in this snow."

"The bugs are enormous and disgusting," he muttered, "and I don't know anyone in Florida."

"You don't know anyone here either," I said, then felt bad the second after I said it.

He didn't reply as he continued to kick at the fence.

"Well, I better go before I say any more stupid things," I added. "Sorry again about the whole spying thing, Lance."

I turned left and continued my boring, dreary walk toward the Petites' house to pick up the twins and get on with my boring, dreary life.

But just then, I heard a scraping noise. I glanced back over my shoulder as the tall black gate slowly swung open, like magic, pushing back the snow. When it stopped, Lance stepped through and stood on the icy sidewalk facing me.

"Ruby LaRue?" he said. "Would you like to come inside my house?"

I had never been inside a mansion before, except for the fake one at Nuzzlenook Farms, where you can have a wedding in the summer by the fake moat filled with fake swans. I followed Lance across the massive snowy front yard over to the giant door.

"I can't stay long," I explained as we stepped inside and removed our boots, "because technically I'm grounded, but also I have to get my little brothers over at the—WHOA!!"

When Lance flipped on the lights, I couldn't believe my eyes. It *was* exactly like a castle! Or what I imagined the inside of a castle would look like. We entered the front area, which was as wide and high as the main hall in our middle school, except this place was a thousand times more amazing, with a floor made out of flat pink stones and walls covered in fancy wallpaper and *four* enormous fairy-tale chandeliers hanging from the ceiling.

"WOWZA!" I exclaimed, way too loudly, then clamped my hand over my mouth.

"You can make noise," said Lance. "No one's here. Not even my governess."

"What's a governess? Is that like a lady governor?"

"She's my teacher, but she also lives with us and eats dinner with me, because my parents are usually busy working or traveling."

Since he'd been so unfriendly for so long, I was surprised Lance was sharing details of his life. He still looked away from me when he spoke, but maybe he just needed new glasses.

"Your teacher lives with you? Why don't you just go to our school?"

"The answer to that is complex," he said, and then crossed his arms.

I wondered what had made him open up like this, and actually invite me inside his mansion. Especially since I had been mean to him. Whatever the reason, I couldn't wait to tell Eleanor all about it.

"My parents had the basement remodeled before we moved in. Do you want to see?"

"Sure," I said softly, like I was dreaming out loud and didn't want to wake up.

I couldn't stop twisting my head around to check out all the awesome rich stuff, like gigantic gold-framed paintings and dark shiny furniture and fifteen-foot-tall windows and statues and vases and a fountain full of water and exactly what you would think a rich family would have in their mansion.

"This is your *basement?*" I said, after we'd taken the stairs to the lower level.

The room was so long I couldn't make out anything on the wall at the other end. Never in my life had I seen so many incredibly fun things to do. There was a pool table and foosball game and two flat-panel televisions. It was like being inside a department store, except it all belonged to one kid.

Lance threw off his jacket and hat, dropped down onto the far end of the cushiony couch, which reclined, and hit a button that made it shake.

"It's a heat-and-massage sectional sofa," he said, his voice jiggling along.

"Cool! Can I try?"

I slipped off my jacket and sat on the opposite end of the L-shaped couch, where a lever released the seat. I found the massage button on the side and pushed it.

"This is the life!" I yelled as my whole body wiggled.

Suddenly, Lance stopped the massager and sat up. Then he stared at me through his binoculars. I turned off my side and popped the lever. It practically threw me out of the couch.

"Wow, Lance! Your house is the best I've *ever* seen. And that includes all the houses in all the TV shows I've ever watched. No wonder you never leave it."

He dropped the binoculars and pushed his glasses up his nose.

"May I ask you a question, Ruby LaRue?"

"Of course," I replied. "Ask me anything!"

At that moment it occurred to me that I felt normal again. As if something deep inside of me had switched on, like this couch massager, and the hundreds of bulbs on the chandeliers upstairs.

"This is what I want to ask you," said Lance. "Why were you sad?"

It was funny he asked me that, at the very same moment I'd started feeling normal again.

"What do you mean?"

"When you walked by yesterday, and again today, both times you appeared sad."

I didn't know what to say. I was shocked he had noticed. Maybe I had been all wrong about Lance, too.

"It's a long story," I told him.

He pushed his messy hair out of his face and sank back into the couch.

"Will you tell me the long story?"

I wasn't sure why he wanted to hear it, but I figured it would be safe to tell Lance everything. He didn't know anyone involved, so it wasn't like he would gossip. Plus, he seemed truly interested.

So I started at the beginning with our visit to Madame Magnifique for our free dream readings and then moved on to my obsession with the Outers and my enormous crush on JB and skiing and E & R Dream Designs and the Deluxe Pluckarama and the Snow Ball and then the accident and getting in trouble with Mim, and then Mr. B, all the way to finding out about JB's secret love notes that were to Eleanor . . . not to me.

After I finished, I realized I had jabbered on for so long that poor Lance hadn't been able to say a word. But even though he stared at the ceiling the whole time, I could tell he had been listening, because he hadn't moved an inch.

"So that's why I've been sad these last few days," I said. "But you know what? Even though all those terrible things happened, my glass is half-full again! I feel much better, thanks to you."

And that's when Lance said the best five words I'd ever heard.

"You can go with me."

I felt my whole body freeze. I took a moment, then spoke in my calmest voice.

"What are you talking about, Lance? I can go *where* with you?"

"The Snow Ball," he replied. "I can take you as my guest if you still want to attend. We can ride in the limo."

Did he just say *the limo?*

It's difficult to describe how I felt at that very moment. My heart started to race so fast I got a little light-headed, and the colors in the room turned blurry. I wanted to make sure I understood *exactly* what he meant, because lately, I didn't seem to be getting anything right.

"*Ohmygosh!* Are we talking about the same thing? The Snow Ball at Sugar Mountain?"

"Yes. My parents usually go every year as a business obligation."

"*Every year?* But you just moved here a few months ago."

"That has nothing to do with it. It's an investment. My parents own it."

"Your parents own *what?*"

"Sugar Mountain."

I'm pretty sure I screamed REALLY LOUDLY at that point, because Lance folded up his legs and blocked his ears. I soared off the couch and landed right in front of him on the fluffy white carpet.

"Are you telling the truth, Lance? Tell me you're telling the truth!"

"I always tell the truth, Ruby LaRue," he said, frowning. "I don't lie."

"WAIT! So, let me get this straight. Are you asking *me* if I want to go with *you* to the Snow Ball at Sugar Mountain?"

He gazed back over his shoulder, which I realized he did when he felt confused.

"Didn't I ask you that already?"

I couldn't help myself! I jumped up and down and up and down and hollered *YIPPPPPEEEEE* as loud as I could.

"Does that mean you want to go with me to the Snow Ball?" asked Lance.

I dropped backwards down onto the soft, luxurious rug, pretending to faint.

"What the heck do you think it means, Lance? Of course I do!"

"But didn't you say those girls, the *Outers*, were cruel to you after you accidentally crashed into them? Won't they be at the party?"

"Well, you and your family used to be Outers too before you moved here, right? And it turns out you're wicked nice, even though I thought you weren't at first. So I'm sure I'll like some of the other Outers there. Plus, it's just so glamorous and exciting—who wouldn't want to go to a real ball?!"

My mind drifted off to dreams of the Snow Ball. All my life I'd seen beautiful photos and articles about the annual event, and now I was actually going with one of the family members who owned the whole mountain! All thanks to Madame Magnifique and her psychic powers.

"Ruby LaRue?" asked Lance in a very small voice. "Are you mad at me now? You're quiet now, like you're mad."

I lifted my head off the ground to look at him. He rubbed his hands together anxiously. His feet were tapping the ground.

"Mad? Nope, I'm the opposite. I'm wicked excited and happy! I'm just daydreaming about it all."

He tilted his head so he could see me through his curly bangs.

"Oh," he replied. "That must be what's causing the problem."

This kid baffled me. Why was it so difficult to talk to him? I sat up and crossed my legs.

"What problem, Lance?"

"*My* problem," he said, and he began rocking back and forth.

"Can you tell me what that problem is?" I asked in the nicest way possible, even though I felt like grabbing him so he would stop rocking.

"Basically, my problem is, I cannot understand people—what they're feeling or thinking. Unless I can see it *clearly*, like a smile."

"How come?" I said. "Do you need new glasses?"

He finally stopped rocking and tapping and fiddling with his binoculars.

"My eyeglass prescription is sufficient. I have Asperger's, officially known as an autism spectrum disorder."

I didn't know what it was, but it sounded serious.

"Is that a disease?"

"It's just the way I *am*. A condition. My governess said I can't read between the lines like everyone else."

"Oh, you mean, like, you're a slow reader? Because I know how that feels. I'm the slowest in my class. It takes me practically a whole year to finish a book."

Lance pressed his fists into his legs.

"No, not that kind of reading," he said.

I could tell he felt frustrated again.

"I don't know what I'm supposed to say, specifically, or how I'm supposed to feel, exactly, when I'm around another person."

I thought about that for a second.

"Do you mean you can't *read people?*"

"Right, I can't read people," he said, and released a big sigh of relief. And then he added, "That's why I'm weird."

I stood up and sat next to him. All at once, everything about Lance made sense.

"It doesn't make you weird. It makes you interesting!"

He shoved his hair away and glanced at me out of the corner of his blue eyes. Once again, I noticed Lance could be a pretty cute guy if he cleaned up a little.

"It makes me interesting?"

"Yep! And now I get why you're so quiet sometimes. There's nothing weird about being quiet sometimes. Plenty of people are quiet all the time. Even my best friend, Eleanor, is quiet most of the time."

And that's when it hit me.

Maybe Eleanor was quiet because she felt "weird" too. And that maybe I made her feel that way when I pointed out and questioned all the different things about her family, even though I only did it because I'm a very curious person.

"Is that why you don't go to our school?" I asked Lance. "Why the governor lady teaches you?"

"Part of the reason."

"What's the other part?"

"We're extremely wealthy and we travel a lot. I would have to change schools often."

I glanced around the basement of this super-rich kid, taking in all the cool things to play with. There were giant Nerf toys, sports equipment, and practically anything a boy might beg for on his birthday. But I also noticed that everything looked new. Even the pool table had a clear plastic sheet pulled across the top.

"Did your parents buy all this stuff recently, for Christmas or something?"

"No, they bought it when we moved in. Why?"

"Well, it looks like no one's played with any of it."

"That's correct. No one's played with any of it, except the video-game systems. I use those every day."

Now I was confused.

"Then why is all this other stuff even here?"

He bit his lip, then stared down at his binoculars and began fiddling with them again.

"My parents bought it hoping I would make a friend."

And that's when I understood how the richest kid in Paris could be unhappy.

"Lance. I'll come over anytime and hang out with you and play with all of this cool stuff, and I bet Eleanor will too, and I can bring my twin brothers who would love to—*oh no!*"

"Oh no, what?" said Lance.

"*Henry and Charlie!* I forgot about them!" I said, pulling on my jacket as fast as I could. "I have to go."

"Are you coming back?" he asked as we ran up the stairs to the first floor and down the long fancy front hallway.

"Definitely. Maybe even tomorrow!" I said, and shoved on my boots next to the giant front door. "I'll call you, except I don't even know—"

And then I stopped and looked right at him.

"What's your last name, Lance?"

He replied, "Charmant."

"Is that French?"

"Yes, it translates to 'charming' in English."

"Charming?" I giggled. "Like *Prince* Charming?"

He squinted at me. "Who's that?"

"Someone who only exists in my daydreams," I said, stretching my mouth into the widest smile I could make. "By the way, my answer is yes. I want to go to the Sugar Mountain Snow Ball with you, Lance Charmant. Thank you for asking me."

And for the first time since I had laid eyes on him, Lance smiled back at me.

"You're welcome, Ruby LaRue."

"Okay, I'm here," said Eleanor, sliding in across from me at our usual picnic table. "What's so *incredible* that you couldn't tell me at school?"

We were back at Dream Central with Henry and Charlie, just like old times.

Except it was nothing like old times. Everything was so much better than it was just yesterday. For one thing, Mim had canceled my two-week grounding, because she couldn't stand the thought of punishing me . . . but more importantly, she had stopped by Mr. B's gas station to apologize about not checking with him before we had started our company.

Mr. B said he understood that Mim was just trying to help, and that he thought I was an excellent friend to Eleanor. Well, that made Mim so proud that she couldn't stay angry any longer.

"I can't believe you're actually here!" I said. "Does your amma know?"

"She knows, and she's fine with it," replied Eleanor, frowning a little. "In fact, she hasn't mentioned my missed activities at all.

And she's said nothing about E and R Dream Designs, even though Thaththa told me she knows about it. She's also acting very peculiar."

"Peculiar? How?"

"I don't know exactly, but listen to this. Yesterday afternoon I discovered her exercising in front of the television. In sweatpants. With the window shades up! When I asked what she was doing, Amma said she had taken Zumba classes in New York and found them *energizing*. Can you believe it?"

"I think that's great," I replied, as I searched the other side of the park beyond where the twins were playing. I was so excited about my incredible news that I was having a hard time concentrating.

"Ruby! If you're surreptitiously seeking a certain seventh grader in a green jacket, I can assure you he'll never be back here again. He knows I'm not—"

"Hey!" I interrupted her and stood up. "There he is!"

Eleanor slowly twisted around. "Oh no . . . *who?*"

"LANCE!" I yelled, waving, as he plodded toward us through the deep snow, his binoculars swaying back and forth.

"Eleanor, this is Lance! The boy who lives in the mansion at the corner of Maine Street and Bon Hiver Lane. We finally met yesterday!"

Lance jammed his hands in his jacket pockets and pulled his hat so low his hair practically covered his foggy glasses.

"Oh," said Eleanor, clearly surprised. "Hi."

Lance mumbled *Hi* back without looking at either of us, then slipped in next to me.

"You'll never believe what I found out about Lance," I said, and grabbed Eleanor's arm. "It turns out his parents *own* Sugar Mountain. Isn't that incredible?"

"That *is* incredible," Eleanor replied. "I didn't know it was possible to own a whole mountain. So is that your incredible news?"

"Yes, but it gets better," I grinned, about to explode with excitement. "After we met yesterday, I told Lance about our psychic dream readings with Madame M, and how it all ended so badly. But then, just like that, he saved the day!"

Eleanor scrunched up her face like she was having a hard time believing all of this.

"He did? How?"

"Lance asked me to go to the Snow Ball with him . . . *in their limo!* Can you believe it, Eleanor? It's even better than my dream, especially after that whole JB disaster."

She didn't say anything at first, then replied, "Wow, that is incredible, Ruby. I'm so happy for you that everything came true."

Even though she was smiling, she didn't seem happy.

"But Eleanor, that's not the best part. You get to go too!"

"I do?"

"Remember? My stepmom has two more tickets from working at the Slope Side Café."

"But . . . I *can't* go."

"What? Why not?!"

"Well, for one thing, I don't have anyone to go with."

"Of course you do! And he'll be here any second."

"What?" Eleanor looked almost mad. "Ruby, don't tell me you—"

"Hey, peeps!" a voice called from the sidewalk. "Don't you have anything better to do than play at a kiddie park?"

Eleanor groaned. "Anton? You want me to go to the Snow Ball with *Anton?*"

But before I could explain, a flurry of snowballs showered down on us from the playground. Lance immediately ducked his head under the table.

"STOP THAT, YOU TWO!" I yelled at the twins. "You know you aren't allowed to throw those at people."

"*Geez!*" shouted Anton, who had received most of the direct hits. "Why are you little twerps attacking me?"

Charlie yelled back with his hands on his hips, " *'Cause you're the creepy kid who's been spying on us!*"

I guess green jackets were popular for boys that year, because it seemed like every boy we knew was wearing one. After all my "green jacket" suspicions, it kinda made sense that Anton would be the spy keeping tabs on Eleanor. It was the kind of goofy thing he would do. Plus, I could tell, he really, *really* liked her.

"You were the spy?" said Eleanor. "Why would you do that?"

Anton finished brushing the snow from his jacket, then asked, "Can I sit down first?"

"Not until you explain," she replied.

"Come on, Eleanor," I said, "Anton was the only person in the whole school who stuck up for me on Monday—let him sit."

She hesitated, then moved to the far end of the bench.

"I wouldn't call it spying, exactly," said Anton as he slid in next to her. "I just wanted to see what you were doing, since you stopped going to Math Squad. But every time I walked down here, I lost the guts to come over."

"Why?" asked Eleanor. "I see you every day at school, and even sit with you at lunch."

"I don't know," he muttered. "I didn't want you to think I was *looking for you* looking for you."

"That's a ridiculous explanation," she said, and frowned.

"Well, I know exactly what he means," I chimed in, "so let's agree to move forward and make some party plans! The Snow Ball is soon, and we've got lots to think about."

But Eleanor said it didn't matter whether or not she wanted to go to a dance with anyone, there was no way her mother would ever allow her to attend.

"Why don't I stop by your house and chat her up?" said Anton. "Adults love me."

Eleanor rolled her eyes.

"Wait! That's not a bad idea," I said. "Or how about *I* visit your house, and convince your mother that it's just a bunch of friends going together."

"Except it's not," said Anton. He pointed at Lance. "Who's that?"

Lance's head was still tucked halfway under the table in case of another snowball attack.

"Oh I forgot—this is Lance, but he doesn't really like to talk at first," I explained. "He has Aspirin-berger's."

"*Asperger's*," barked Lance, as he popped into view. "And I didn't give you permission to tell people."

"It's no big deal," said Anton. "My little sister is an Aspie, so I know all about it."

Lance studied him out of the corner of his eye and asked, "Are you an Aspie too?"

"Not that I know of," Anton said, smiling.

"You never told me that you have a sister," said Eleanor. "Is she okay?"

"Of course she's okay," said Anton. "She's practically a genius."

"A genius like you, Eleanor!" I said, and grinned. "Anyway, I apologize about that, Lance. But can we get back to the reason we're all here? The Snow Ball's in just sixteen days, so we have to get your mother on board, ASAP. Why don't I stop by your house on Saturday, Eleanor?"

Eleanor didn't look convinced.

"Ruby, you know how my mother is."

"What's wrong with your mother?" asked Anton.

"Nothing," she replied quietly. "She's just traditional, from another country. It's hard to explain."

"Sounds like my parents," said Anton. "They emigrated from Russia before I was born, but they still have all these annoying rules no one else has."

"Really?" replied Eleanor. "That's exactly how mine are too."

"See?" I said. "Something you have in common! Plus, you just told me how much your mother has changed since she's been back. So I'll just drop by your house and pretend the two of us are going to do homework, even though we only have gym together, but they don't need to know that. And then I bet your father will invite me to stay for supper."

She sighed. "Whatever. I guess we have nothing more to lose."

Lance suddenly spoke up. "Bring flowers."

"Good point," said Anton. "Women love flowers."

I corrected him. "*Most* women like flowers, Anton."

He glanced at Eleanor.

"Do you like flowers?"

"They're okay," she said, shrugging her shoulders like she didn't care, but I could see a tiny ribbon smile starting to form.

By the time I rang the doorbell at the Bandaranaikes' on Saturday, my bouquet of mint-green carnations from the grocery store had flopped under the frigid temps. Mim had supplied me with another hostess gift, but this time it was a basket of fruit.

"I'm not sure this is going to work, Ruby," said Eleanor, who stood at the front door, shivering.

"Why not?"

"I don't know. My mother has definitely changed in some ways," she whispered, "but I'm not sure how she feels about spontaneous visitors, or my friends coming to—"

"Who's there?" a woman's voice called from inside the house.

Eleanor puckered up her face.

"It's me, Mrs. B," I called out as cheerfully as I could. "Ruby LaRue! Just stopping by to study and do homework."

Eleanor's mother appeared at the door wearing one of her silky Sri Lankan outfits.

"What is all of this?" asked her mother, taking the flowers and basket of fruit from my hands.

"A little something from me and my stepmother. We know you've been gone a long time, so it's a 'welcome back' gift!"

"How very considerate. Well, you must come in, please," said Mrs. B, in that same plucky way Mr. B spoke. "It's quite cold today."

Without being told, I removed my snowy boots at the door with dainty, ladylike manners, and slipped off my jacket to hang on the coatrack. It dawned on me that a lot had changed since the previous Saturday when I had lain facedown in this very spot, bawling my eyes out.

"We have had our tea, Ruby, but may I fetch a cup for you?"

"Yes, thank you, if that wouldn't be too much trouble."

Eleanor shook her head at me as if this was all a terrible idea, but I was determined to win over her mother. I knew I had only one chance to get this right, and I didn't want to blow it. So I would be as respectful and polite as I could possibly be.

"Are we really going to do homework?" she whispered.

"We have to at least pretend," I said.

"In my bedroom?"

"No, out here where she can see us, so we can chat."

Eleanor moaned.

We sat down on the family room floor in front of the crackling fire and spread our books across the coffee table.

"How do you like your tea, Ruby?" asked Mrs. B, poking her head into the room. "With sugar and cream?"

"However you think is the best way to drink it, Mrs. B."

"Very well," she replied, and smiled, disappearing back into the kitchen.

"Ruby, I'm not even sure I want to go to the Snow Ball—it's your dream, not mine."

"What do you mean?" I whispered, but I felt like grabbing Eleanor's shoulders and shouting. "This could be the most fantabulous thing we ever do in our lives. Besides, my dream isn't complete unless my very best friend in the whole world is there with me."

"But Ruby, how can you still want to go after the way those despicable girls treated you?"

"Just because a few Outers were awful doesn't mean all of them are," I said. "Plus, I've realized I don't need to be an Outer to have an incredible time at an incredible party with my own incredible friends!"

Just then, Mrs. B reappeared with a wooden tray.

"May I offer you a piece of fruit from your lovely basket, Ruby?"

"No, thank you," I said. "Those are all for you."

She set the tray on a side table, poured the tea into a delicate cup, and placed it in front of me.

"Tell me, where did you learn such lovely manners?" asked Mrs. B. "Your parents have raised you well."

"Thank you," I replied, smiling as hard as I could. "Actually, I'm practicing really hard for a fancy event I'll be attending."

Eleanor cleared her throat as if warning me to change the subject.

"What event is that?"

"The Snow Ball," I answered carefully, "up at Sugar Mountain."

"Ah," she said, nodding. "I thought that was a party for adults who winter in the condominiums?"

"Oh no, lots of kids go . . . although it's mostly for the rich Outers who ski, but a few local people go too. And it's not like a date thing at all—it's more of a fun *group* thing, so we're going as a group, me and some friends."

I peered over at Eleanor, who was watching for her mother's reaction.

"Except," I continued, "I have this one friend who would love to go too, as part of our group—and she has a free ticket and everything—but her parents probably won't allow it."

Mrs. B sank down into the comfortable chair.

"I can understand their reservations about such an event at your age," she sighed, "but has she asked her parents yet?"

Eleanor shifted nervously and said, "You probably don't want to hear this, Amma. It's silly school stuff."

"But I do!" said her mother.

"Are you sure?" asked Eleanor. "It will just upset you, and then you'll ask a million questions."

"Why do you think that?"

"Because . . . ," she stammered, "that's the way you always are . . . about everything."

Mrs. B tilted forward in her chair, as if she might get angry, but then she smiled.

"That is not true. I know I've been reluctant to accept the way of life here," she said, "but your cousins in New York helped me to understand that your generation is as much American as we, the older ones, are Sri Lankan."

And right then I understood exactly how Eleanor must feel, getting pulled back and forth between two worlds, never belonging fully to one or the other.

"Really, Amma?" she said. "Even if you knew that *I* am the friend who wants to attend the Sugar Mountain Snow Ball?"

Just as Mrs. B's jaw dropped to the floor, the back door swung open.

"Hello there, Ruby!" said Eleanor's father. "I didn't know we were expecting company."

"Hi, there, Mr. B!" I said, and jumped to my feet, anxious to change the mood in the room. "It's so good to see you. Eleanor and I are doing a little homework and drinking delicious tea here with Mrs. B."

But Eleanor's mother still didn't look happy. She stood up and waved her hands all over the place.

"I do not understand what is going on in my own home—I'm gone a few months and suddenly my eleven-year-old daughter wants to attend an adult *revelry?*"

I didn't know what that word meant, but I knew it didn't sound good.

"Tell me," said poor Mr. B, trying to smile, "what is this all about?"

"Eleanor wants to go to the annual dance up on the mountain," cried her mother, "at night—with strangers, and *boys!*"

"You see?" said Eleanor. "I knew nothing had really changed, Amma. Already you are saying no!"

"*Please*," said Mr. B, clasping his hands like he was about to pray for help. "Let's all calm down and talk about this together."

The room was so quiet you could have heard a snowflake hit the ground outside, which is where I wished I was at that moment, since I seemed to have made everything a hundred times worse.

Eleanor stared down at the floor now, like she might start to cry.

Mr. B frowned, while Mrs. B took huge breaths in and out.

"Eleanor," said her father, "please tell us how this all began. Why do you wish to attend this event?"

Eleanor straightened her back and sighed.

"I want Ruby to tell it."

Now all eyes were on me.

At first I thought that was a bad idea. In fact, I was just about to leave so the Bandaranaikes could sort out this mess among themselves in their own way. But then Mrs. B gazed at me with such sad eyes. I could tell she really wanted to be part of Eleanor's life, but didn't know how to do that without going against everything she believed.

And then I thought about how bad Mim would feel if I didn't share things with her. I mean, not everything, but most things, because that's what made us close.

So I sat back down on the floor and began at the beginning—like I did with Lance—the day we saw mysterious Madame M's poster. Except this time I chose my words very carefully, explaining how we never thought we were doing anything we shouldn't be doing, which was mostly true.

After Eleanor's parents heard the entire story—Madame Magnifique's predictions, my goal of becoming friends with the Outers and going to the Snow Ball, Eleanor's dream of developing her own fashion line with that fancy sewing machine she wanted so badly, the rise and fall of our company, my disastrous day trying to ski (but leaving out the part about Eleanor receiving secret admirer notes), and Lance's offer to host the four of us along with safe transportation in their family limousine to the dance—Mr. and Mrs. B said nothing for a long time.

A *very* long time.

Finally, Eleanor's father spoke.

"Thank you, Ruby."

"No problem," I said, and glanced at Eleanor, who sat frozen like a block of ice. "I mean, you're welcome."

"Eleanor," asked Mr. B, "did Ruby tell us everything?"

Eleanor nodded.

"Then your mother and I shall go to the kitchen and discuss what we have just heard. Will you both please wait here?"

After they exited the room, I leaned over and whispered, "*Wow*, you were right when you said your house is just like a courtroom. This feels exactly like Judge Jennifer on channel twenty-eight. It's kind of exciting."

"Thanks for trying, Ruby," she replied, "but my mother will always be traditional and stubborn, and my father will always let her decide in the end."

I felt awful about pushing Eleanor to go to the Snow Ball and interfering in her life. I understood now that different families and cultures have different ways of doing things, but that didn't make one way better than the other.

Her parents soon reappeared. They stood over us as Eleanor and I huddled together on the floor by the coffee table. Our school books, untouched, were piled neatly in front of us. I took a last sip of tea from the little bit in the bottom of my cup, but it was cold.

"As you know, we wish we had been informed of your endeavors," Mr. B began, "however, we admire your resolve, Eleanor. And we already know that Ruby is a very good and trusted friend."

"And so is Eleanor!" I blurted.

Her father nodded, but he didn't smile. Her mother studied the wall on the other side of the room, her arms crossed tightly.

I had such a bad feeling about all of this. What if I'd truly made everything a hundred times worse? What if Eleanor would be scheduled even more now, with no free time ever again?

"However, one very important question remains," added Eleanor's mother.

She turned and faced us, her hands now planted on her hips.

This was it. I felt like I had to say something before Eleanor was sentenced to house confinement for the rest of her life, but I couldn't think of anything.

Eleanor peered up. "What is it, Amma?"

"Exactly what do you two girls plan on wearing to such a glamorous event?"

I *gasped* as if I had just won the entire Showcase Showdown from Bob Barker himself!

"Are you saying I can go?" asked Eleanor.

Her mother grinned.

"Yes, you may go, Eleanor. But we must meet these other friends in your group *and* the driver of the limousine."

We both jumped up and hugged each other, then I hugged her parents, who looked surprised. I heard Eleanor whisper, "*Sthuthi* . . . thank you, Amma and Thaththa."

"Guess what!" I said. "My stepmom and I are going shopping next weekend if you want to come with us. They're having a huge winter clearance sale over at the outlets in North Conway."

"That's very considerate of you, Ruby," said Mr. B, "but, please, I have a much better idea."

A minute later, Eleanor's father returned, carrying a gigantic cardboard box that blocked his face and most of his body.

"An early birthday present, Eleanor," he said.

"But my birthday isn't until May," she said. "Is it from New York?"

"I have no idea what it is," said her mother. "This is news to me, too."

Well, I could not believe my eyes . . . and neither could Eleanor. It was exactly what *she* had been dreaming of: the Deluxe Electronic Pluckarama 1080 Sew-Good & Embroidery Machine!!

It was as if Madame Magnifique herself had waved her wand and made it appear.

Eleanor could barely get her words out.

"*But*—but how did you know, Thaththa?" she asked.

"You mentioned the name of the machine," said her father, "last weekend, when I learned about the business enterprise you two had developed. I ordered it online that night and it arrived yesterday."

"Oh, Eleanor," I said, "you can design and make your very own fabulous dress for the dance."

"And for you, too, Ruby—the one you wanted in the catalog! I still have the sketch."

"Oh no, not in such a short time," I replied. "I can shop with Mim at the mall."

"You will not get any old factory dress at the mall," said Mrs. B. "I am happy to help with the sewing while Eleanor is in school during the day."

Then she squeezed between the two of us and draped her arms around our shoulders.

"You two girls will have the most beautiful dresses at the Snow Ball!"

The following two weeks were a blur of preparations, but before we knew it, our big day had arrived!

Somehow, Eleanor and her mother had made the most gorgeous dresses I had ever seen on that fancy sewing machine. Mine was pure white with fake fur around the neck, and tiny clear buttons down the front that "twinkled like stars at night under the lights," just like the picture in the catalog. And Mim bought me these fancy new silver wedges that matched the gown perfectly. Eleanor's dress was made from a creamy silky material that was simple and plain on the hanger, but looked amazing once she put it on, prettier than anything I'd ever seen. Definitely *haute couture*.

The night before the Snow Ball, I had set my clock to wake me up extra early so I would have all day to get ready. As it turned out, I didn't need an alarm, because the best two words in the entire world woke up the whole house just before sunrise.

"I'M HOME!!"

Within seconds, the four of us were on top of Pop, hugging and kissing him until he could barely breathe. He said he wouldn't have missed my first dance no matter how much they paid him. At first, Mim couldn't stop crying she was so happy, but then the twins whined that they were hungry, so she calmed down and made banana pancakes.

I spent the day catching up with Pop and getting ready for the Snow Ball. Later in the afternoon, Eleanor and her parents drove to our home so that everyone could meet each other. Everyone got along really well, and Eleanor was amazed when she saw our house.

"How come everything is so neat and organized?" she whispered in my ear as the grown-ups chatted at the kitchen table.

"I told you I've been doing a little at a time, like you said, and somehow it got a lot better."

Eleanor announced she had a surprise and ran outside to their car. I assumed it was something for me, but it was a gift for Mim.

"For you, Mrs. LaRue . . . a thank-you for donating all of your supplies to E and R Dream Designs. Without your support, our dreams never would have come true."

Well, I'm telling you, Mim started to cry like a baby all over again, just as she had that morning. This time, she bawled so hard, Pop had to hold her tight and pat her back to get her to catch her breath.

"I apologize," she cried. "I'm just so darn *happy* that everything's worked out for everyone."

Inside the perfectly wrapped box was a crocheted pink beach robe dotted in tiny flowers with a long matching belt. It looked exactly like something the real Marilyn Monroe would have worn.

"Oh, Eleanor," said Mim, "this is the prettiest thing I've ever seen. I'll wear it every single day by the Aqua-Pedic this summer."

"Or at the new bakery," said Pop. "That'll really attract the customers!" he added, and laughed.

Everyone fell silent.

"What new bakery?" I asked.

Mim sniffed back a few more happy tears.

"Oh my," she said. "I didn't want to hog your super-special day, girls, but we do have a very big announcement to make."

"Good news, I hope?" asked Mr. B.

Pop wrapped his arm around Mim and said, "Excellent news!"

"You see, the reason your dad's been away so long, and that we've both been working extra hard and cutting corners these past months wasn't just to save up for the aboveground pool," said Mim, now looking directly at me. "Your pop and I are opening our very own family bakery in the village!"

"For real?" I gasped.

"Yep!" said Pop. "It's about time Mim made her own profits on those famous Monster Chunk cookies of hers."

I couldn't believe it—even Mim's deepest dream had come true.

"Congratulations to you both!" exclaimed Mrs. B. "Have you leased a location yet?"

"Well, it just so happens," said Mim, "that the perfect space is available right across the street from the playground at Winterberry Common where the boys like to play. Won't that be convenient?"

Eleanor and I looked at each other and said at the same time, "Dream Central!"

"Dream Central?" repeated Mim. And then her eyes practically popped out of her head. "You know what? That's exactly what we should call it—*Dream Central Bakery!*"

It's funny how things can seem fine one day, then not so good, then really amazing, followed by horrendous, and then back to fantastic. But in the end, I couldn't help wondering if Madame Magnifique had had something to do with the way everything had turned out.

All at once the twins began hollering, "It's here! It's here! *The LIMO is here!!*"

All eight of us instantly turned and ran for the door, clogging up the exit as we tried to squeeze out at the same time. Somehow we managed to gather on the front porch just as the limousine pulled in front and parked. It was long, black, and very shiny!

I felt my arm being squeezed. It was Eleanor, grinning wider than I'd ever seen her smile. We grabbed hands and squealed, "*We're going to the Snow Ball!!*"

The driver, wearing a dark coat and hat, went around and opened the door.

Anton stepped out first, followed closely by Lance. Both boys were dressed in white, which is the color everyone wears to the ball, white like snow. Best of all, they had wrist corsages made of pretty white flowers for us, which I had never even heard of, but Mim said that meant they were true gentlemen.

Anton acted like he was in charge and shook hands with the adults and gave lots of compliments to Eleanor in front of her parents, while Lance hid behind the open limo door, staring down at his feet. But

I didn't mind, because I knew that's where he felt comfortable. Plus, I noticed he'd gotten a haircut, which meant he was trying hard to look extra nice. I was glad I could finally see his whole face.

Mim took about a hundred photos of Eleanor and me, then Anton and Eleanor, then Lance and me by the limo, then the four of us by the limo, then Eleanor with her parents, then Eleanor and me and Marilyn, the old cat, with the twins, and—well, you get the picture.

The sun was starting to set behind the frosty, purply-blue mountains, so it was time to get going.

"Imagine," Mim said to me as she held my shoulders, "you, *Ruby LaRue*, are going to the Snow Ball with the son of the owners of Sugar Mountain. What a world!"

"I guess anything is possible," I said, and kissed her cheek, "if you believe it's possible."

Mim threw her head back and laughed.

"You know, I'm so impressed by the wonderful young woman you're blossoming into, Rosebud," she said. "Your real mother would be too."

I leaned in and gave her a hug.

"You're my real mother, Mim," I whispered, "and you always have been."

"Oh goodness," she cried, "now don't get me bawling all over again!"

As we drove away from the house, all four parents waved and waved good-bye to us, like we were never coming back, even though we would be home in a few hours.

I guess there are some things I'll never understand about grown-ups.

Crowds of people were lined up all along the road to Sugar Mountain, watching us like we were royalty or something. The limousine slowed down and stopped just before the old Sugar Tree near the entrance.

Eleanor and I locked eyes.

"Do you think JB will be here," she asked me, "with an Outer?"

"Probably, but who cares?" I said. "We're VIPs! Isn't that right, Lance?"

"Yep," he mumbled. "We can even sit at the head table if we want."

Eleanor and I grabbed each other again and shrieked for about the tenth time that day.

"I could get used to this," said Anton, as he took another sparkling apple cider from the tiny refrigerator.

So many people were arriving at the dance at once that a traffic jam had formed. The line crept slowly forward as guests pulled up one at a time in front of the main lodge. I rolled down the window and stuck my head out to get a better view.

Everything was more beautiful than I'd ever imagined. Every tree glimmered under sparkling lights, and long white carpets ran up and down the sidewalks, and all the way to the top of the steep flight of stairs.

When our driver finally pulled up to the drop-off area, he rushed around the limo and opened the door for us. He held my hand and then Eleanor's as we stepped out carefully and gracefully—as if we were real-life princesses.

Photographers took pictures of all the beautiful people arriving, and one woman even asked Eleanor and me to pause and pose for the newspaper! I had spots in my eyes from the flash, so for a minute I couldn't see anything. But then Anton got bossy as usual and told us to follow him, which was a good thing, because I was dizzy from the *fabulousness* of it all.

I turned to grab on to Lance to help me climb the staircase in my fancy new silver wedges, but he was nowhere to be seen.

"Where's Lance?"

Eleanor pointed. "I think he's down there by the bushes."

"I'll get him," said Anton.

"No, it's okay," I replied. "I will."

Lance's arms were crossed tightly in front of his white blazer and he seemed to be shaking. It was chilly outside, but I didn't think the temperature had anything to do with it.

"Is this hard for you?" I asked.

He shoved his hands in his pockets. That's when I noticed his binoculars were missing, and I wondered if he felt more anxious without them.

"I know you don't want to be here," I said, "and that you're doing it all for me. But this has been so much fun already, Lance, it's fine if you want us to turn around and go home now."

He peered up at me.

"It is?"

I nodded.

"I'm not sure if I can go inside."

"Well, if you want to try," I said, "I promise to stay right next to you the whole night."

He gazed up the steep flight of stairs, at all the people dressed in white gowns and tuxedos, the cameras, the decorations, the music, the lights. Above it all, the moon was full and frosty and stars filled the sky, twinkling magically over the sugary peak.

I reached out and he took my hand.

Once all four of us were inside the front entrance, Lance relaxed a little.

For one thing, practically everyone on the staff knew who he was and seemed eager to take care of us. It was hard to believe, but we really did have reserved seats at the awesome VIP table, along with about thirty other important guests. That meant we got to sit up high on a platform in front of the entire crowd.

I have to admit, I had been nervous all day about bumping into those mean Outer girls, wondering what I would say. But now that I was at the ball, gazing across a sea of fancy gowns, I realized they wouldn't be wearing their ski jackets, hats, and goggles. So I wouldn't recognize any of them even if I tried—not even Page, the unfriendly ski instructor!

Every single person was dressed up in the most beautiful shades of white, from their outfits to their shoes and accessories. And the inside was even more spectacular than the outside, with millions of tiny clear lights and shimmering decorations bedazzling the entire ski lodge.

Eleanor told me she had been wicked nervous too, but mostly about seeing JB. It turned out he was there, but not as a local guest like us—JB Knox was working as a busboy! His arm was no longer in a sling, but he still wore a brace. We spotted him as soon as we sat down at the VIP table.

Throughout the first course, a yummy creamy soup, I noticed JB sneaking glances across the room at Eleanor. So after the next course, a sweet salad with fruit and nuts, I convinced her to go over to the other side where he was working and say hello. I mean, it really didn't make sense for everyone to stay mad at each other. Especially on such a magical night.

As we ate our delicious entrées, a choice of steak or lobster, Eleanor told me she had found out JB had been working a few hours every week at the lodge all season, because it was the only way he could afford to join the ski club. And, like Mim, he got two complimentary tickets as an employee. But he said he didn't want to go to the Snow Ball after Eleanor turned him down, so he had signed up to work it instead . . . never in a million years expecting to run into her.

I knew that seeing JB waiting on the Outers, instead of flirting with them, made Eleanor think twice about how she felt. That maybe JB wasn't as arrogant and selfish as she had judged him to be. I realized even I had overreacted to the way JB had treated me. I mean, when I thought about the bunny slope incident, everyone else had been yelling at me about crashing into JB, but not him.

The whole meal was scrumptious—four courses in all! I almost died when I saw the dessert cart: everything you could ever dream of, including a huge variety platter of Mim's famous Monster Chunk cookies.

Between each course, Anton had mingled a lot, talking to everyone like he does at school. I wouldn't be surprised if he ended up owning Sugar Mountain someday.

But Lance didn't leave his chair all through the meal, not until later, when the floor was cleared and the band started to play. That's when he surprised me again, by asking me to dance! That kid was one big surprise after another. Turns out, dancing is one of his favorite things to do.

Other than JB, we didn't see anyone else from school at the Snow Ball . . . but it made me realize something very important. The Outers could have been anyone from plain old Paris. They laughed, ate, and talked to each other just like ordinary people do every day, all over the world.

Eleanor was right. Being able to afford fancy clothes and stuff didn't make them better or happier. Finding happiness is the same for everyone—it can only come from the heart.

Shortly before midnight, the time we'd promised our parents we'd end our evening, I insisted we warm up by the large fireplace before heading out into the cold. The night had been perfect, but I wasn't quite ready to leave.

After collecting our coats, the four of us sank into the large couch and placed our feet on the warm stone hearth. The crackling flames danced magically in front of our eyes.

A waiter appeared, carrying a tray of mugs, and asked, "A cup of hot chocolate before you leave?"

Across the room I saw JB clearing dirty dishes from a table.

"We'd love some," I replied, and held up my hand. "Five, please."

Finally, my dream felt complete.

Several days after the dance, the Petites invited the twins to spend the afternoon with their grandson, Jean-Philippe, who was visiting from Québec. It turned out Eleanor was free after school as well, since her mother no longer scheduled every minute of her day—not that she let Eleanor drop *everything*, but at least she had loosened up and allowed her to make some of her own choices.

Ms. Duncan rushed over to our lockers as we zipped up our jackets and loaded our backpacks. She was holding a clipboard.

"The first Paris Middle School Ping-Pong Club convenes tomorrow, girls, and I want the co-captains to be on time."

"We'll be there," said Eleanor.

"Three p.m. on the dot!" added Ms. D as she hurried away to the next gym emergency.

"Got it, Coach!" I called down the hallway.

I had never called anyone *Coach* before, but I liked it.

Both Eleanor and I had been pretty surprised when Ms. Duncan asked us to be on the new team, and totally shocked when she asked us to be the captains. But it felt good. It made me realize—

like everything else we'd been through lately—that a lot of stuff you think will happen doesn't, and stuff you never thought would happen does. So it's best to be open to anything and everything life throws at you, because you never know where it will take you next.

As we followed the crowd of kids toward the exit through the old wooden doors, I heard Mr. Tankhorn's voice above the commotion.

"Haven't seen you in a while, Ms. LaRue."

He was standing by the cafeteria, blowing his nose.

"That's because I'm not tardy anymore, Mr. T!"

"Happy to hear that—they won't put up with those shenanigans in high school!"

A half-foot of snow still covered the ground, but little signs of spring were everywhere. The days were much longer now, and birds sang from every tree.

We decided to walk into the village and stop by all our favorite places, starting with Dream Central. Someone was sitting at our old picnic table, which bothered me at first, but Eleanor pointed out that it would happen more often now that the weather was getting warmer. It was time to share it with others.

Across the street, we noticed the carpenters and painters working away on the new bakery, which was due to open as soon as Pop finished his last cross-country haul. Now he would be home all the time, working for Mim, his new boss.

We also dropped by the Treasure Chest to visit with Mrs. Wilder, who begged us to start up our business again, which we were thinking about doing over summer vacation, since Eleanor's parents had agreed it would be okay—as long as it didn't interfere with her brainiac activities and cello lessons.

Afterward, we moseyed over to The Avalanche, but unlike the old days when I would have polished off a large mocha ripple milkshake all by myself, Eleanor and I shared a raspberry yogurt smoothie instead.

As we sat at the little round table, sipping our pink drink together, Eleanor pulled something out of her pocket and showed it to me. Two notes.

"One for you. One for me. They were at the bottom of my locker."

I unfolded the tiny yellow paper and read it out loud: "Hi, Ruby. I want you to know I am not that person you crashed into at Sugar Mountain. It was an accident, and I shouldn't have let everyone blame you. I'm sorry. I hope we can be friends. JB Knox (P.S. Thanks for the hot chocolate by the fire.)"

I still wasn't sure how I felt about JB, but I knew it took a lot of guts for him to write an apology like that. So maybe he would never be the love of my life, but at least we could try to be friends. I mean, who couldn't use another friend in this crazy world?

"What does yours say?" I asked Eleanor.

She grinned like she was too embarrassed to read it, but I reminded her of the promise—that there would be no more secrets between us. She read: "Dear Eleanor—You were the prettiest girl at the Snow Ball. Maybe next year you'll go with me? If not, Anton seems like a nice guy. I hope you two had a fun evening together. NA."

"Aww, you should go with JB . . . that note is so sweet and wicked romantic."

"Maybe," she replied, "but I actually had a good time with Anton."

Then Eleanor grinned and asked, "How about you, Ruby? Are you going to the Snow Ball again next year?"

I couldn't help giggling. "Lance said he would take me every year for the rest of my life."

"Aww, *that's* so sweet and romantic!" cried Eleanor, and we laughed until we couldn't laugh any longer.

After finishing up the smoothie we hurried off to our last stop, Wonderland's Used Books. Eleanor immediately beelined over to the front shelf to check out the latest arrivals, while I wandered over to the community bulletin board.

And that's when I saw it.

"Pssht, Eleanor!" I said, exactly the way she does when she wants my attention, except I think everyone in the store must have heard me.

Eleanor glanced over and squinted.

"Look!" I whispered as loudly as I could through my cupped hands.

She dropped her armful of books back on the shelf and rushed over.

I was *so* excited, I practically shouted the words out loud:

TODAY ONLY
ONE FREE SESSION WITH
"*Madame Magnifique*"
THE WORLD'S MOST DIVINE PSYCHIC
DISCOVER YOUR TRUE PATH IN LIFE BY UNLOCKING
YOUR DEEPEST DREAMS!

I'm telling you, the two of us *squealed*, then tore out of that store and down the sidewalk, turned right where the Dumpsters usually stood (but were mysteriously missing again!), past the wooden sign that read Apparition Way (which was mysteriously hanging again!), and up the mushy-snowy alley without saying a single word to one another.

We arrived in front of Madame Magnifique's glowing entrance at exactly the same moment, both of us puffing large clouds of frosty breath into the bright, cool air.

"*Bonjour, les filles!*"

"*BONJOUR!*" we yelled together.

She was dressed exactly as she had been before, red feather and all, except she appeared shorter. But maybe we had grown a little taller?

"*S'il vous plaît*, come in, girls. *Vite, vite!* I have much to tell you."

We followed her down the same narrow hallway (that still smelled like warm gingerbread) to the same table in the same back room, melting in golden light and velvet, exactly as it had been back in December!

"And you are—*who?*" she asked, tilting her head to one shoulder.

I was surprised she didn't recognize us.

"We were here just a few months ago," I said. "Don't you remember? You told us our deepest dreams."

"I see many, many faces, and you do look familiar. Did you want a refund?"

"No, our readings were free!" Eleanor blurted. "Plus, our dreams came true, just as you predicted."

Madame M grinned. "Well, then, what can I do for you today?"

"For one thing," I said, "we want to thank you for helping us with your magical powers."

"It is my pleasure!" she said, her cheery cheeks blushing a deeper red. "Of course, I am pleased, but not astonished."

"But also, Madame M," I continued, "*where in the world have you been? We've checked back, like, a hundred times, looking for you! We had so many questions and wanted your help."

"Hmm, I do not know what you mean," she said, pushing her bottom lip into a pout and scratching her forehead. "I had to make a stop for a manicure this afternoon, but then I returned here about a half-hour ago."

Eleanor and I immediately turned to each other in amazement. Back in December, she had also mentioned a manicure appointment. What was going on?

"*Mais, les filles!* Since we were successful the first time, may I suggest new *drrream* readings, free of charge?"

Without skipping a beat, we both cried, "*Oui!*"

As before, the psychic began to hum loudly like a swarm of bees, and then gazed up at the ceiling, reaching her arms up overhead. Everything was a strange repeat of what had occurred at our first visit. Then she suddenly cut off her humming and arm-waving with a big smack on the edge of the table.

"*Maintenant,* I want you to place your hands flat, and you must lock your thumbs like this."

We immediately copied her, our hands shaped like birds.

"Now, close your eyes and say these words: *Stars and moons and worlds that beam, lead me to my deepest drrream!*"

Staring at one another—half-scared, half-silly, as we had been the first time—we repeated the chant.

"*Ouvrez!*" she cried, and blew out the candles. "Open!"

The same sweet smoke clouded the space in front of us and Madame Magnifique squeezed the top of our bird-shaped hands . . . just as before.

"You!" she began, staring at me. "Once your creativity is unleashed, there will be no stopping you from realizing your fullest potential and achieving your deepest *drrream*."

I felt my mouth drop open—not because I was amazed, but because I was confused!

"And you!" she said, now facing Eleanor. "In order to unlock your deepest *drrream,* you must go outside your world, to the unfamiliar, reaching far beyond your comfort zone."

The exact same predictions as last time. *Only reversed?*

Madame Magnifique lifted her hands and blew across her fingers and palms like she did before, as if scattering magic dust.

Eleanor and I were in shock. We said nothing.

Could it be there had been no magic at all? No destiny? Was Madame Magnifique just a phony act?

Was it possible that we had achieved our goals all on our own?

We followed her back through the narrow gingerbread hallway and stumbled out the alley door into the late-afternoon light.

"Thank you," we said at the same time.

The dream reader winked as she gave a tiny wave with the tips of her fingers.

"*Rêvez bien!* Dream well," she replied, "Ruby and Eleanor."

ACKNOWLEDGMENTS

This novel has journeyed through several transformations. I'm grateful for the valuable input and suggestions of many people, especially Shannon Barefield and my agent, Susie Cohen. My deepest thanks to Melissa Kim, my editor at Islandport Press, who believed in this story and knew exactly how to shape it. Also, I want to acknowledge Rushani Perera at the Sri Lankan Embassy in Washington, DC, for verifying Sinhalese terms and cultural questions, as well as Valerie Jensen, who reviewed the French phrases, and copy editor Melissa Hayes for her keen eye and kind words. And I want to extend a warm hug to the Chandraratne family and most of all, to Padmini Chandraratne, my generous, loving host mother and friend from the exquisite island country of Sri Lanka, where I spent a life-changing college semester (and left a piece of my heart) so many years ago.

ABOUT THE AUTHOR

Elizabeth Atkinson, the award-winning author of *I, Emma Freke*, believes in the magic of stories to transform lives. She's enormously proud of her twenty-something children, Madeleine and Nathaniel, and her husband, Erik, who runs his own cool company and the Hot Chocolate Motorcycle Gang. When she isn't writing or reading, she's probably out and about exploring with her best friend, Obadiah, the amazing doodle dog. She divides her time between the north shore of Massachusetts and the mountains of Maine. Elizabeth visits schools all over the country, virtually and in person. Find out more: www.elizabethatkinson.com.